I0822610

Covid 19: An Extraordinary Time

Covid 19: An Extraordinary Time

an anthology

Edited by Debz Hobbs-Wyatt and Gill James

Chapeltown Books

British Library Cataloguing in Publication Data

A Record of this Publication is available from the British Library

ISBN 978-1-910542-72-9

This edition published 2021 by Chapeltown Books
Manchester, England

Contents

Introduction

We invited trusted writers who are published by Bridge House, CaféLit, Chapeltown and The Red Telephone to submit texts they created in 2020 whilst the world grappled with Covid 19. They were also invited to ask their trusted writing friends to do the same.

All of the works here have been edited but only lightly. We accepted all submitted pieces. We would have made more than one book if need be. So, we have a rather large book but we're glad we were able to fit all of the suggested pieces into one volume.

We've arranged the works in date order so they reflect any changing mood. Only in order to accommodate a formatting issue such as having a poem on one double page spread instead of including a page turn have we deviated from this a little.

This is a souvenir book. It is one writers may want to bury in a time capsule. You're probably reading this because you are or you know one of the contributing writers. This offers a partial record of a truly extraordinary time – hence our subtitle. We felt it needed documenting but not merely in descriptive prose, as Samuel Pepys did in his diaries, which describe some equally challenging times, but in all sorts of other texts, texts that show the creativity of their authors.

Another book is also in production: *Aftermath.* This again is a commissioned souvenir book and explores the new normal. We held submissions open until we had fifty texts. All were accepted and again are being edited.

As I write this, Covid 19 is tightening its grip in an ugly second wave. We are rolling out vaccines but there is still some way to go. Maybe we shall need to produce more volumes. Certainly we feel duty-bound to record these times which continue to become more and more extraordinary.

Gill James January 2021

March

Thinking About Contamination

Dawn Knox

I have an idea for a product to combat COVID-19.

When I finally make it, I'll call it COViolet.

It's not intended to kill the virus nor to promote an antibody response. It's simply a dye that once applied, will turn virus particles vivid violet.

COVID-19 will no longer be invisible.

Violet colouration on a door handle, ATM or petrol pump will warn everyone of contamination.

If there's violet colouration on your fingers, don't touch your face. Wash your hands thoroughly for twenty seconds.

COViolet doesn't exist yet.

Until it does, why not treat EVERYTHING as if it were violet?

Two Meeters

Stuart Larner

After the Prime Minister's broadcast
I became very fat.
I measured a metre more all round.

Going out, I wore
A giant ball of nothing.
The heaviest nothing I ever had.

I smiled with others, learning how
To manage awkward nothings,
Each keeping a metre to make two.

Though only our boundaries can meet
Nevertheless
Some part of us reaches through to the heart.

Who Is at Risk?

Colin Payn

It was Sainsbury's Happy Hour. A time slot for the pensioners and care workers to enjoy exclusive access to the depleted shelves of a nation under coronavirus curfew. A time to wave to friends from two metres away, if you recognise them in their makeshift masks. Was that a vintage B&Q dust filter? Or an up-to the-minute Screwfix model?

A genuine NHS issue indicates a hero from the front line, whilst a knitted scarf, however colourful, really won't hack it.

Plastic gloves, plastic bags wrapped over trolley handles, shoppers being careful. But till operators? No masks. Why?

Pandemic

Janet Howson

I reflect on my side profile in the full-length mirror. I feel enormous now. My belly is hard and shiny like an outsize conker, a reminder to me of my vulnerability. To be expecting a baby during the coronavirus, just my luck. A worry I did not need.

I move away from the mirror and put my T-shirt on. I will ring my mother later. She is self-isolating, she too is vulnerable.

I sit down and study my list of proposed names for the baby.

I could always call her Pandora. It is a pandemic after all.

The Return of Mothercare

Colin Payn

2021 should have been a year of celebration as countries recovered from Covid-19. The ability to go to supermarkets without queuing or rearranging meals depending on which aisles were empty. Being able to go for a drive without being stopped by the police. Holidays at home or abroad. Hands not raw from frequent washing. Hugging friends and family. Parties and BBQs.

Everything looked wonderful, who knew how good life was up to 2020? The word on everybody's lips was, 'FREEDOM'.

Almost everyone's lips. Not women in their forties, or with teenagers, or careers.

Victims of the Post Virus Baby Boom.

Adding My Thoughts to the Virus Fray

Hannah Retallick

March 17th 2020

I wasn't going to share anything publicly about… we all know what! I'm more of an introspective writer, not often commenting on wider issues such as politics and, well, pandemics. It's not because I don't care – I write about them privately – but more because I *don't know*. I read all sorts of articles, see conflicting views from experts, and non-experts like me, and don't feel in all conscience that I can share anything. Why should I throw my 'opinion' into the mix? This jumble of words started to flow this morning though.

Coronavirus responses from the general public: isn't there a middle ground between panic and apathy? Unfortunately, panic and apathy shout the loudest, throwing people from one extreme to the other. News and social media love extremes – extremes get clicks. I suspect the 'truth' is somewhere in between, and that's not me hedging my bets and sitting on the fence (*cringes at the two overused expressions*).

Many of the extreme views come from only looking at one aspect of the situation. For instance, it's all very well saying that only a small percentage will die, as if that's the only issue here. It's no comfort to an already-strained health service and people with other medical conditions; it's no comfort to people who might lose their jobs and essential income; and it's no comfort to people whose small businesses might not recover.

People feel helpless, because in many ways we are. We don't know exactly what will happen. I'm a planner, and I find it difficult that all bets are off. (Wow, I'm killing it with the clichéd metaphors today!) We can never be sure what the future holds, but we're now in a situation in which trying to make any kind of plans seems impossible. Not only are people scared about what this means for their jobs and health, they have also been told to avoid 'unnecessary' recreational activities – activities such as playing in a brass band, which are lifelines for some people.

In times of crisis, there's an inbuilt desire to *do something*. Washing your hands, avoiding touching your face, and staying at home when possible doesn't feel enough. So, people stockpile. Yes, this might be a response motivated by selfishness from some… but it's also motivated by fear. This has a ripple effect. People who are taking a more measured approach now have to consider whether they should buy one more pack of *insert item here* because their stocks are low and they don't want to be faced with an empty shelf once they've run out. Supplies must be taking a hit from that too. (Side note: I feel sorry for large families, whose weekly shops must look like panic buying.)

As somebody who has a tendency for anxiety, I'm used to dealing with crises inside my own head (!) and have developed ways to deal with external crises too – well, mostly. I'm not worrying about contracting the virus, but I'm concerned for more vulnerable people, as we all are, and would hate to pass it on. I'm currently in a privileged position where I can easily 'self-isolate' – as I like to joke, I'm inclined to do that anyway! (#introverthumour) I also have my postponed dissertation to distract me, which now seems like a blessing.

I'm trying to confine my 'consumption' of the news/social media, to reduce the brain chaos and create some semblance of calm. I'm also attempting to see the good in each day, and to create as much good as possible, for myself and others.

My dad likes to say, "If you can do something about it, do it; if you can't, then there's no point worrying." Of course, that's far easier said than done, but it's worth remembering. There's plenty we can do to help others and shine light on the situation, through praying and taking positive action – supporting local businesses, supporting elderly people etc. Thank you to everyone who is beavering away and sharing ideas and tips with others – these positive things can have a ripple effect too. I'd love to hear more about what you're doing, so please leave a comment.

Panic and apathy aren't the only options. Our responses make a difference. It's just that sometimes it doesn't *feel* like it.

Lots of love at this difficult time.

From a non-expert who finds it therapeutic expressing her thoughts in writing.

Two Metres Apart… Or Not!

Joy Mawby

By Benllech beach. 6.40 am March 26th 2020

The little elderly man was hovering round his car with his fat old corgi. I'd often seen them both hobbling along the beach, sometimes with his wife in tow. I had finished my dog-walk and stopped two metres away from him and asked, "Is everything all right?"

"I can't open the car door. I think the fob battery is flat."

He held the fob up once more, pressed it and the door opened. He and the dog got in, I put the dogs in my car and then realised the man was beside me once more. I took two steps away.

"It won't start," he said. "It's fully automatic so if the fob's battery goes, nothing works."

"Have you a phone with you?"

"No."

I realised I hadn't brought mine either. "If you tell me your phone number," I said, helpfully, "I'll go home and phone your wife and tell her what has happened. Have you got roadside rescue insurance?"

"I'm with Green Flag."

"Your wife could call them, couldn't she? They'll come and sort you out."

"My wife is fast asleep. The phone never wakes her." He came closer to me again and I moved away.

"Could you do me a really big favour? Could you run me home?"

What could I say? I couldn't just leave him and go home for breakfast, could I?

"Yes, all right, I'll take my dogs and drop them off and come back for you immediately."

I returned within five minutes. He was standing by his car with a mobile in his hand.

"I found it in the glove box, after all," he explained, "and my wife heard it ringing so she knows I'm on my way."

He *found* his phone and his wife woke up when it rang? I thought. But I said nothing, of course.

I had to lift the dog into my car as its legs were too short to jump in. I sat well over to the right of the driver's seat but, even so, we were practically touching, the man and I. He told me the way to his bungalow – about a ten minutes' drive. His wife was standing by the gate in a pink fluffy dressing gown as we drew up. She came over and handed him the key fob.

"I just need to go to the toilet," he said, getting out and I realised that they expected me to take him back to collect his car.

Well, what could I say?

"You are kind," the wife said to me, popping her head through the car window. I recoiled. "Oh sorry," she exclaimed, stepping away. "I keep forgetting the safe distance rule. Would you like to come in for a cup of tea?"

Walking in the Time of Corona

Lesley Hawkins

JEN: So… daily digi journal entry – March 26th 2020:

Trying to think what to say about this most recent experience. Where to start? Generally, regarding the current social distancing situation all I can think of to say is, "Yippee I'm off work!" I love my jobs but still, who wouldn't want to have a bit of enforced leave? Recharge the batteries and all that.

I'm a lucky duck, Dad is currently well and being sensible, I still get to keep fit and go in the garden and pop to the shops if I'm careful and I am careful, I've a personality which is a bit jobs-worth with stuff like this. "Step away if you know what's good for you!" *(Laughs.)*

So I'm using gloves and handwashing like a mad thing, I've a strict personal 2m rule in place. If someone comes too close I literally stop breathing and my fight or flight instinct buzzes around like a shut-in dog when the postman delivers. Not afraid to do wide circles around folk in order to maintain the distance.

Wish others could get it too, do some of the work, make being outside less stressful.

*****

CHERYL: Bloody hell. Fucking cheek of it! Still can't get my breath! Oh for goodness sake! Where ARE you? *(She fiddles with her phone then chucks it on the floor.)*

HELEN: *(A voice emanates from the phone.) Hey, hey! You OK? What's up? (Cheryl grabs the phone, sees her friend and promptly bursts into frustrated tears.)*

*****

JEN: But, getting back to the point, dear journal, a couple of days ago we were out for a walk, him and me.

Considering how down he's been the past year that's something really positive.

Yeah, very recently he's even been initiating the walks again, getting outside. Baby steps but nevertheless baby steps in the right direction. Hah! See what I did there? Walking, steps…?

*****

CHERYL: *(She's recovered slightly and is speaking in animated fashion to her friend.)* Annoying man! How dare he tell me what to do. Patronising sod! If I see him again, I'll, I'll… I'll set Denver on him!

HELEN: *(Laughing)* now you're being ridiculous. What's up, what's happened to get you so cross?

*****

JEN: So there we were, comfortable in our own company, chatting quietly, walking along a lane near the woodland entrance to what had been a favourite walk of ours, when we spotted dog walkers standing across from each other on either side of the lane. They were also chatting. Enough distance between them but, fight or flight is starting to kick in now, not enough room for us to walk through comfortably.

It was a couple on one side of the lane and a woman on her own on the other. Think I've already mentioned that both had dogs, suppose that's beside the point, but never mind.

I mentioned my concern to him and as we got closer; me desperately hoping a miracle would happen, that they would just spot us and move or magically disappear or… something!

Him that's with me, opened his mouth and suggested that due to the current situation they might be better standing on the same side of the lane to chat. Still 2m apart obviously but giving others access to safe passage along the lane.

Well!

*****

CHERYL: …told off proper I was. Just been for a lovely walk with Denver, stopped to chat to Jane and Dez and this guy out walking with a woman said didn't we think that considering the current situation it might be better if I moved to the other side of the road? Fucking cheek!

I think the woman tried to say something as well but I wasn't listening to any more crap! There was loads of room, well not loads, but enough I reckon.

Don't need this with what's happening with our lad at the moment, just wanted a bit of normality, nice walk, out with the dog. NO HASSLE! So I told this guy what I thought of him and his idea.

*****

JEN: The guy from the couple got what we were saying and I'm there trying to smooth the waters over, trying to be reasonable. I've been incredibly touchy about bugs since Mum contracted sepsis, made her last years on earth difficult to watch especially when I couldn't visit cos I wasn't well. Hate it even now when a colleague brings a cold to work. Just want to stay safe and keep others safe too. So I was just trying to reiterate what he'd said but in a careful soothing way. To no avail. And as we walked away we heard ourselves being violently berated.

*****

CHERYL: (Thoughtful silence, a few beats then…) Did I over react?

I over-reacted didn't I? [sigh] I do get this distancing thing, think it'd just slipped my mind for a second in all the 'normality.' (*She laughs unenthusiastically.*)

HELEN: Probably. Understandable though, you wanted to enjoy a walk out without being hassled or worried. I get it. But you're always so worried about how Joe's feeling and what he's going to do next. Depression, is a horrible thing, Cheryl, and too much for one person to deal with without support. Don't get me wrong it's great that you're there for him…

CHERYL: He's my son. I couldn't not be. Could you? Just wish it didn't leave me feeling so edgy all the time.

HELEN: But being on constant alert like you are, you need to look after yourself and this was just your way of letting off steam. I bet they'd understand if they knew.

*****

JEN: I was a bit pissed off being shouted at, at the time, I think we'd been reasonable in our request. Anyhow it gave us something else to talk about all the way round the woods but once I'd calmed down I realised that we don't have a clue what someone else is going through, you never know, she might have been a carer like me, so I'm now recording it in my mindfulness journal. To remind me not to be such a judgy arse in the future.

Extract from Covid 2020

Roger Noons

Day 9 – Sunday 29 March

Drastic measures, *The Archers* omnibus has been reduced to an hour. The PM told us it would get worse before it got better, but he never said it would be this bad. Bloody cold as well this morning; six degrees, feels like one. No chance of working in the garden.

Not wanting interference in my creative pursuits, I've never owned a TV set, which reminds me of an occasion many years ago when I was addressing a group of *Young Wives* on the subject of preventing accidents in the home. I happened to say that I didn't have a set following which the Chairlady asked, "What do you do in the evening?"

I told her, "I talk to my wife." There followed a long silence.

I have found myself watching more and more iPlayer, movies on Amazon Prime and YouTube and with the deliveries from Majestic Wine, I wonder if I shall ever write anything else ever again. Exactly why I never bought a telly.

Socially Distant Runners

Hannah Retallick

March 31st 2020

Yesterday, Mum and I took our precious daily walk along a main road with beautiful mountain views. We kept a careful look-out. The social-distancing (physical-distancing) thing is strange; it feels odd to deliberately avoid people, even for an introvert like me! It's better to be safe than sorry though.

As we were walking, a young couple came up behind us. We stepped through an open gateway into a field to let them pass and then crossed the road to avoid an oncoming pedestrian. The woman had to pull her dog and pram onto the sloping verge because the young couple didn't move out of the way, despite having an empty road to their right! They stayed side by side, dawdling, and didn't seem to acknowledge her in any way. She wasn't happy.

I got irate from a distance. Two older friends have said recently how they keep seeing people in their teens/twenties flouting the social-distancing rules, and although I know so many of us are doing what we can to keep people safe, it's frustrating to witness. There was no excuse. (I know it might seem a small thing, but… even in 'normal times', you shouldn't force a mother, baby and dog off a path. Just sayin'.)

Anyway, I walked the same route today, feeling a little cranky and anxious. Grey sky, drizzle, should have worn a coat.

An oncoming runner turned back as soon as I came into view, bless her. I heard something behind me, looked over my shoulder, and there was another young woman running.

She slowed her pace while she was still a few metres away and said, "Oh, sorry."

"No worries, I'll cross the road," I said, before she lost her stride. "Oh, actually, I can walk right in the middle of the road! This is so weird, isn't it?"

She laughed as she passed. "Yeah! Thanks very much."

"No worries, have a good one."

"You too!"

The exchange made me smile again. Young people redeemed themselves... and they didn't do runners' reputation any harm either.

April

Join Me

Mary Daurio

Our world spins, drunk on fear. My friend, Bill, says, “Stop! Don’t come near.” As we call from the walk, screaming to talk, I realise he’s scared shitless. Good job, toilet paper is now a commodity.

Medical treatment does its part. Unfortunately, some folks’ silliness is beyond healing.

Our human race, friendships too, have survived cataclysmic events, and with science and faith, we will withstand this as well.

Bill flings a paper plane. Its message, ‘Come join me for a pint of Corona when they lick this virus, and the world regains stasis’.

I holler, “Your house or mine?”

Something's Happened to the Humans

Gill James

The humans are behaving oddly. Some of them have stopped putting out those delicious fat balls and those exquisite black seeds at the feeding stations they make for us. And they're going to their own feeding stations less. In fact, they're only going to the ones where they carry the food back to their nests. They're not leaving their nests so often either.

A lot of them are covering their beaks with things that make their beaks look more like ours.

There aren't so many of their machines rattling along their flight paths but there seem to still be plenty of those that flash dark blue and light blue. And the humans that come out of them are wearing feathers over their ordinary feathers as well as the beak-masks.

Maybe it's like what happened to us a few moons ago – when some of us started falling out of the sky for no reason.

I expect they'll get over it. We did.

The sun's still shining. There are plenty of worms and insects and juicy vegetation this time of year. We don't really need their feeding stations.

Best leave them to it.

After all, there are nests to be built, eggs to be laid and very soon youngsters to feed.

There is something else though: the air tastes a lot sweeter as well.

The Silent Slayer

Ella Etienne-Richards

Please understand that it's lethal
We don't know where it lies
Waiting, ready to pounce
It's a sly and silent terminator

Be alert, be vigilant.
Don't let your guard down
It's ruthless and shows no mercy,
It does not discriminate.

Thousands have fallen prey to it
And thousands more will
Be aware that no one is immune
But here's hope, we can defeat this.

Cover your mouth when you cough,
Wash your hands, Wash it out,
Into the bowels of the sewers
Where this filth really belongs.

Your friends now are your enemies
It hides and lies in wait
Always hungry for a new host.
Stay away from each other

It's now a matter of 'life and death'.
Do not give it the ammunition it needs
Act now and Act swiftly,
Save yourself and those around you.

Self-isolate, for your sake and others
Help those who are vulnerable
But at a safe distance.
Our world is under attack

By a serious deadly infestation
Stop the nonsense, be sensible.
Put a stop to Social Interaction
Social distancing is paramount.

We must all play our role
To stop this mass murderer
Death is all around us
Do the right thing now.

Don’t be afraid, Be Positive,
Let’s work together
At a safe distance
To vanquish this Silent Killer.

Brian

A.S Charly

Absorbed in his mobile game, Brian grabbed a beer.

"Yuck!"

Glass shattered.

The next morning, two scientists entered the laboratory and found a broken vial in front of the cooling unit.

"Jeez… how often did I tell this dumbass night guard that this is not a fridge!"

The other scientist rolled his eyes. "Brian again. I really thought he had understood after the flu incident. Can't we get rid of him?"

The first scientist raised his eyebrow. "That's illegal."

"I meant fire him."

"Unfortunately not. Equality and all that…"

They both sighed.

"Let's see if we can avoid another pandemic."

Green Shoots

Last year's undergrowth was still in the process of rotting away. There were crab apples lying in piles under the hedges. Up on the moors there were clumps of non-descript brown grasses with bulrushes interspersed among them waving in the wind. It had been a mild winter, so the grass had continued to grow but most of it had been eaten off by the sheep.

Further down in the valley, there were splashes of colour from the holly growing in the hedges and ivy clinging to the trunks of trees. Soon it would be spring. Primroses would appear by the brook and then wood anemones. There were already catkins dangling from the hazel bushes and she'd seen at least one pussy willow tree.

There was only one road out of the village so you could either walk uphill or down. Whichever way you chose, you still had hills to contend with. Uphill led you to the moors. It was a hard climb uphill all the way. Once you got to the crossroads, you could sit on the bench, provided by the local council and survey the scene. There was more traffic up here, going in four directions. It would be people on their way to the shops, mainly. All non-essential travel had been stopped, because the local beauty spots kept getting clogged up with traffic.

When they were young, they'd once thought of setting up a stall by the roadside here and selling stuff. It had never come off. Her mother would never have allowed it, not after that time when she'd been caught selling rosehips at school. Enterprising, she would have called it, showing ambition and drive. Instead of which she'd been put it the corner like a dunce.

It was a beautiful spot, with the Ribble Valley splayed out below, framed by the distant North Pennine Hills. This had been her uncle's favourite walk. He used to come up here every day after lunch, when his wife was having her afternoon nap. It was what kept him going right into his nineties. She didn't think she'd live that long. That generation were made of sterner stuff. They'd lived through the war.

A woman walked past pushing a pram with a baby in and an infant running alongside, trying to keep up. They greeted each other, keeping their distance. These were unusual times. A flock of fieldfare flew overhead. At least that was what she thought they were. She wasn't an expert on birds, by any stretch of the imagination. There was a curlew calling somewhere in the distance. She heard them every day. It must be the nesting season. They usually flew around for a while, warning people off and then settled back on the nest when they were gone. Otherwise you just heard the crows, and seagulls that had migrated inland in search of food.

She liked the silence. It took you out of the mundane. It helped you clear your mind, so you could focus on the essential things. A bit like doing meditation or mindfulness. At these times, you could think more deeply. She was glad she'd got out of the city when she did. If she'd stayed, she'd have been stuck in a one-bedroom flat with no garden to sit in and nowhere to get away from it all. She felt privileged to be living in a place like this.

She would go back home the field way. She climbed over the stile and set off across the field to the wood that ran beside the brook. The Rivers Trust had recently been planting new saplings here to restructure the landscape and halt the flow of water. They would serve the dual purpose of absorbing carbon dioxide from the atmosphere and stopping the planet warming up so much. Hopefully that work would continue in the future. It was early days, but it was still important to contemplate a future.

She passed the reconverted barn, let out to holidaymakers in summer. They probably wouldn't be coming this year. There was another stile to climb and then she was in the field, the one they used to ski down in winter when they were kids. They'd made the skis out of an old wooden barrel and tied them on to their feet with bits of wire. It was a wonder they hadn't broken their legs. Their mother had seen them out of the kitchen window, but she hadn't stopped them. Such fun they were having.

Walking down the hill they called Long Shoot, she was in full view of the house. There was the Park and Dean Field and the meadow they called Carring. Their names had been imprinted on her memory since childhood. If she veered off to the left, she'd come to the stepping stones across the brook. The ramblers had wanted a bridge built, but her father had been adamant there had never been one and had fought a lifelong battle with the local council over it. She'd rarely seen him so passionate about anything. Maybe that was why she'd never followed that path for fear of upsetting him.

The blackthorn blossom was coming out. It gave the hedgerows a ghostly quality. Their white blossom came out before their leaves, unlike the hawthorn, which was the other way around. Its white and pink blossom followed the leaves. But that was later in May. The old rhyme came into her head: "Cast ne'er a clout, till May be out," which, according to her auntie, referred to may/hawthorn blossom rather than to the month of May. By the looks of things, she wouldn't be casting any clouts just yet.

If you looked closely enough, you could just make out green shoots appearing in the hedgerows and on trees: on the blackthorn, the hawthorn, the hazel, the alder, the ash and the oak. Another bout of fine weather and they would be bursting into life. Whatever else was happening, you couldn't stop spring.

Eyam

Vanessa Horn

Silently, Emmot stood waiting with the group of villagers – some physically in attendance, others spiritually so. She stared up at Rector Mompesson on his elevated hill-spot. Why had the new preacher gathered everyone here today? Surely, at this terrible time, his duties should be tending the sick and dying rather than summoning the surviving villagers to a meeting? No wonder he wasn't proving popular if this was how he was behaving.

After a short time, the clergyman held up his hand and the people fell silent. Emmot continued to stare, her mind churning. What would he say? What *could* he say?

Mompesson's voice was quiet. Calm. "Residents of Eyam, thank you for coming here at this time of devastation. Many people have died. Many people are suffering. For these reasons, I know that you will agree it is time to act. That we must attempt to stave this pestilence which has overtaken our village." He paused, looking down. Around. At his flock.

"But what can we do, Rector?"

Emmot turned. Jane Riley. Two children lost and a husband ailing, the older woman was in tears. "Nowt we've tried has worked."

Mompesson nodded. "This is true. However, although there is no remedy yet, there are precautions which could, God willing, prevent the disorder from spreading further."

Emmot frowned. What possible *precautions* could wipe out this deadly disease? A disease which turned the victim's skin black, that produced buboes in their groin and caused uncontrollable vomiting?

"Firstly, we need to avoid being confined indoors together. To minimise breathing the contaminated air," Mompesson continued. "With this in mind, therefore, we will meet regularly here, outside, at Cucklet Delph.

Secondly… we will have to bury our dead in gardens or fields from now onwards – the demand for graves in the churchyard is too high."

Emmot startled as angry oaths and curses erupted from the crowd around her. She silently thanked God that her own mother had been an early victim, with no question of being buried anywhere other than the churchyard. But what of the rest of the family, if they should perish?

Mary Peters – three children lost – spoke. "Rector, how can our loved ones be accepted on Judgement Day if they are not buried in consecrated ground?"

Mompesson sighed. "It is a huge sacrifice, Mistress Peters, but God himself will surely understand." He waited.

To gauge *their* strength or *his* own, Emmot wondered?

Then the rector drew his shoulders back. "Lastly, and most importantly, we need to isolate ourselves from neighbouring villages to avoid spreading the plague elsewhere."

Emmot gasped. Isolation? No! How, then, would she be able to see Rowland? Her fiancé's daily visits from neighbouring Stoney Middleton were her lifeline – her salvation.

Her thoughts agitated, she listened as Mompesson talked of how goods from other villages would be left by the Boundary Stone. The Eyam folk would put down their money – disinfected in vinegar – at the same spot, therefore enabling them to sustain themselves adequately. She shook her head as she realised that this decision had obviously been resolved long before the concept had been presented to the villagers. The deed was so obviously done.

The rector concluded. "Already, a quarter of our population has been lost. If we can stop the disease spreading to others, our sacrifice will not have been in vain."

Later, as Emmot walked home, her mind spun with frustration and confusion. She couldn't – no, she *wouldn't* – stop seeing Rowland. The idea was inconceivable. This was a sacrifice she was unable to make.

That evening she waited impatiently for her fiancé to arrive, ready to vent out her frustrations. Hoping, against hope, that he would be able to think of a way in which they could continue to see each other. However, as minutes turned to hours, there was still no sign of him.

Seeing her eyes flicker to the window yet again, her father shook his head. "Rowland will know of Mompesson's decision by now, Emmot. He won't be coming."

"No – he won't let me down!" Suddenly resolute, Emmot jumped up, rushing to the door and wrenching it open.

Holding her skirts out of the mud, she ran across the damp fields, through the overgrown glades and down the twisting paths until she reached the river dividing Eyam and Stoney Middleton. Pausing to catch her breath before journeying over the footbridge, she suddenly heard a familiar voice.

"Emmot! Thank God you came!" Rowland was standing on the opposite side of the river, his face a mixture of expressions. Relief? Sadness? Emmot couldn't tell. She was just about to cross the bridge, when Rowland held up his hand.

"No – don't come over!"

Emmot felt the tears prickling her eyes. "But…" She stopped, lost for words.

Rowland continued. "We cannot go against Mompesson… this is the only way we can still see each other, even if it is at a distance."

Emmot thought for a few moments. With a choice between not seeing Rowland at all or meeting with a chasm in between them, she would have to take what she could. This is the way it would have to be. Reluctantly, she nodded. "Every evening, we'll meet here?"

Rowland's voice was steady. "I swear we will. Until this ordeal is over and we can be properly reunited in person again. Also…" here he paused, still gazing intently at his fiancée, "…from tomorrow, I think it better if we don't use our voices. It's too much of a risk."

Emmot felt a numbness wash over her. Not hear her Rowland's declarations of love? Not hear the words which had the power to take away a little of the hardship and starkness of her life? She shook her head. "But surely we won't be heard if we meet further down the river, away from where folk come to wash their clothes?"

"Voices carry though," Rowland replied. "We cannot risk being discovered, for if we are, we will have nothing, not even the sight of each other."

The next evening, as Emmot regarded Rowland across the river, she realised – even more than before – how important their meetings were to her.

Earlier in the day her younger sister Lydia had complained of a headache, and Emmot had feared the worst – that this seemingly innocuous symptom was the start of the plague. Waiting until the little girl was in bed and being looked after by their father, Emmot had run down to the river, desperate to see her fiancé. Even though she could not express her anxiety to him in words, she found that just gazing at him, at his loving smile and kind eyes, gave her the courage to continue. To return home and face whatever God saw fit.

Several days passed and Emmot was reaching a stage where she felt she couldn't bear what her life had come to any longer. Not when she was sitting by the side of an infant who now failed to recognise her big sister and who cried out in agony with the throbbing buboes spreading over her small body.

The hours were a progression of sadness and despair. Emmot's father was little use or comfort to her, having sunk into a deep depression from which he seemed unlikely to rouse. Yet, despite her troubles, Emmot continued to experience a brief respite in the evenings, and knew that without this, she wouldn't be able to cope.

A week elapsed. Lydia died, her tiny body unable to stand the pain any longer. Emmot and her father buried the little girl in the back garden, asking God for His blessing and a swift passage to Heaven for the child. Afterwards, they looked down at the small mound, carefully avoiding each other's eyes and pain. There was nothing to be said. Nothing to be done.

Often, as Emmot was walking slowly home from meeting Rowland, she tried to remember what life had been like before the plague. Before her world had gyrated into a frenzy of illness, death, despair. Was she really the same girl who used to sing as she worked in the house with her mother? The girl who would plait the hair of her little sisters and intertwine daisies into their long locks? She didn't feel as if she was that person anymore, or ever would be again.

It was only during the evenings when Emmot allowed herself the luxury of dreaming. She permitted herself to think forward to the time when the plague would die out, the restrictions would lift, and she and Rowland would be able to reunite in person. They would get married, set up home together. Maybe even have children of their own. It would happen. Wouldn't it?

In his heart of hearts, Rowland knew, without being able to admit it fully to himself, that his and Emmot's time together was limited. That the unrelenting plague which had claimed so many villagers would not wait indefinitely for his beloved. Why would it spare her, when so many had not been granted that luxury? Despite this, he tried to keep positive. Optimistic. After all, she hadn't yielded to the illness yet – surely that was a good sign?

However, on a chilly day towards the end of April, when there was no Emmot waiting for him by the river, Rowland knew. Knew beyond hope. And the stark shock of realisation seemed to freeze his thoughts and emotions, apart from one – the understanding of what he must do.

Walking slowly into the river, Rowland welcomed the rushing current that pushed and shoved against his limbs. He allowed himself to be drawn and dragged beyond his capabilities and powers, submitting to what must be. Finally, he smiled, murmuring, "I'm coming, Emmot," before letting the freezing water overwhelm him.

Parasite

Linda Lewis

With every minute that went by, he could feel his strength fading. If he didn't find a host soon, he would die. Tomorrow morning, would be too late.

Then he saw his prey – a young girl with long brown hair. She was still a long way off but every step brought her closer.

Nearer and nearer she came until he could smell her scent and see the smoothness of her clean white flesh. Her looks didn't matter to him; all he craved was her lifeblood.

He stayed perfectly still, concentrating hard, willing her to come within striking distance. Until that happened, there was nothing he could do.

"Come to me," he breathed.

The hunger pangs were unbearable. If he didn't find a host soon, he would die, his life wasted.

He watched as the girl bent down, plucked a flower from the hedgerow and stopped to breathe in its perfume.

"Don't turn back. Come closer."

Just as he was about to give up hope, she strolled on, humming tunelessly, swinging her arms by her side. When her hand brushed against the undergrowth, he made his move. It was another hour, maybe more, before she touched her mouth.

As he entered her bloodstream, he trembled with pleasure. The next stage of his life cycle could finally begin.

Covid Chat

Cathy Leonard

Since Rosy joined the WhatsApp group…

There have been alerts about thousands of pounds
Flying out of customers' accounts, mostly Danske customers,
But maybe you too…

Preventative cures for Covid-19: like lemon in hot water
Imbibed in the evening with a teaspoon of baking powder…

Images of a Scarlett O'Hara eat-your-heart-out ball gown replete with petticoat hoop—
The latest seasonal-social-distancing outfit from Amazon…

O Corona sung to the tune of Rodgers' and Hammerstein's *Oklahoma*…

Bored lockdown victim cutting the grass with scissors (I do that anyway betimes)…

Dog on strike in protest on top of kitchen cupboard
Refusing to go for yet another inessential outing…

A hundred admonitions to stay safe, wash hands, cough/sneeze into tissue,
Keep two metres apart…

Rotterdam's Philharmonic Orchestra performing
separately-together from different locations…

Good jokes, bad jokes, wine jokes
Did I tell you the one about…

Eight Things Happy People Do…

A clip from the Bee Gees video *Stayin' Alive*…

And a quote from Seamus Heaney:

"If we winter this one out
we can summer anywhere"

Thanks Rosy!!

Lock Down

Cathy Leonard

for my son

We didn't candle-bless your birthday this month.
And Mother's Day has slipped by unkissed and unhugged.

No one's buying Easter eggs and when I see them there
Stocked and shelved in empty aisles I think of you—

Giant Dairy Milk panic-bought early and often
At half price after the event. You
Cracking eggs well into the summer.

This year you text:
Has Easter been cancelled?
Where are we on the graph?
Can we flatten out the curve?
When will it peak?

When can you come home?

Covid in the Park

Cathy Leonard

Ribbons flutter on the path up ahead. Another doomed tree?
Or a wishing-tree, a fairy-tree, a rag-tree?
Repository of our prayers, our requests for intervention,
for blessing in these new Covid days?

Pink and striped, the ribbons look like crystal sugar sticks
Their hydraulic action excavating and demolishing milk teeth
Souvenir rock wrapped in plastic that creaks and cracks and cuts like glass
I smell salt on the air, hear the flow and backflow of waves shingling across stone

But these are Exercise Stations, not trees,
Their candy-striped-pink supplications
Asking you not to embrace
Warning you not to engage

Reminding you that taste and touch
Can be fatal these days.

Covid Talk

Cathy Leonard

Well I'm going down the road anyway! I want to smell grass, feed ducks in the park.
Me too!
You know it's not allowed now. It's illegal.
Since when? Says who?
The government, and if we're caught there'll be consequences. Fines. Maybe jail, and there are hundreds of people there, all sneezing and coughing and spitting on top of each other.
I spat on twenty people last week. Before the lockdown.
I spat on a hundred.
I went out as a bin bag and hopped along the whole length of the road.
You saw that on a video.
Didn't.
Did.
Who says we're unfit? Obese?
Non-essential.
Shouldn't be allowed in shops.
I bought twenty packets of toilet roll, forty cans of pears, six boxes of ice cream and rubber gloves. Dozens of them.
I bought hundreds of hand wipes and Easter eggs and pasta and hand sanitisers.
You can't get those anywhere.
I have loads of them. Thousands.
I want to go to the park. I need fresh air.
We could borrow Rover, next door.
Hates us.
Doesn't.
Does so. Remember that time you nearly killed him.
Thought those pellets were treats.
Did not.

Did.
More like rat poison. He remembers that. Mutts never forget.
That's elephants.
You're allowed brief exercise within two metres of home.
You mean kilometres.
Not us.
Unfair.
Ageist.
I want to cut the heads off daffodils in the park.
With a sword.
Or a stick.
A walking stick.
Berate dog walkers with dogs off leads.
Or on leads.
Throw sticks in the spokes of cyclists.
Trip up joggers.
Get justice!

Voice from the side: **Are you two playing two metres apart?**
We are, Ma.
Well come in and wash your hands and you can have ice cream and pears and then we'll go to the shops, but you know you'll have to—
Stay outside. We know, Ma. We will.

Weathering Covid

Cathy Leonard

This is the summer for aging, for letting it grow grey

For what reach of hand can span two metres and touch and not touch scalp?

And silent, bar the babble of social platforms and doom and fake news

And recalcitrant with once familial passers-by

And virtual in our dealings with each other

Cultivating new friends like cloud and spring bud

Sprung out of storm and withering bough

And hope that we too can weather this tide.

There's an R in...

Roger Noons

"Typical," Jack tutted. "Human beings don't have the brains of a house sparrow."

Rook frowned.

They each looked to Raven who was resting up the corner. His mind seemed far away, but in fact he was concentrating on a smidgeon of meat stuck in his beak. Hedgehog, he thought it was, but you can never tell when it's been flattened by an eighteen-ton-truck.

"Do you agree, Raven?"

"Sorry, Daw, what are you on about?"

"Human beings," chipped in Rook. "Mixing up Covid and Corvid. We have an R, but you cannot expect them to know or take the trouble to check."

Raven and Jackdaw looked at each other, both nodding.

The Silence Outside

Mitzi Danielson-Kaslik

It’s so silent outside
on the streets below
the house that lead
down to the sea that
crashes against the
cliffs and rocks and
eventually ends in
silence like everything
else in the world now
that the streets
outside are in silence
a silence that seems
unbreakable, it’ll be
broken by a single word.

Coronavirus

Michal Reiben

We are on our way home from a holiday in Cambodia; the plane is flying among the clouds. As it dips downwards towards Hong Kong Airport my ears plug up. I feel the plane shudder as it hits the runway and comes to a stop. We descend the stairs. Cold air hits my face and I can smell diesel. We enter the terminal, the building is built from glass and concrete, underfoot the silver tiles gleam. Plasma screens of arrival and departures times hang from one of the walls. All around us I see a sea of irritated faces covered in masks. A stewardess also provides us with masks and we are herded like sheep into an empty part of the terminal. My stomach churns with worry. The thought of being forced to wait all day for our connecting flight in this crowded place where everyone is wearing masks isn't pleasant.

Arriving back in Israel, I am sick with a bad case of flu, my body aches, I'm burning with fever, I cough, sneeze and I'm clogged up with phlegm. Have I caught the new strain the coronavirus or a more common variety? I rush off to a first aid station and explain to the receptionist I want to be checked for the coronavirus. Terrified, she immediately runs away and disappears. After a while, a male nurse wearing a mask appears and addresses me from a safe distance, "You have to go to a hospital and you must wear a mask," he calls out. I buy a packet of masks at a pharmacy and drive off to the local hospital. The two guards at the entrance of the hospital are built like boxers with tattoos displayed on their arms.

"Why are you wearing a mask?" one of them asks. When I clarify the reason, he says, "Don't enter the hospital, wait here."

They both rapidly retreat into the hospital like frightened rabbits. After a short while, a female doctor and her assistant, both wearing masks, turn up. The doctor looks too young for her job, her untidy hair is scooped back in a low ponytail. She professionally looks at me as I explain why I've come.

"Please accompany me to the parking lot outside so you don't contaminate the hospital," she said.

In the parking lot, she commands, "Lift your sweater."

The nurse hovers nervously nearby with knitted brows. The doctor examines my chest and then the nurse takes a sample of my blood and saliva, I stand there feeling gloomy. Cold rain sprinkles on my face and exposed upper body, so that drops of water trickle down me. Coldness creeps over my body and I tremble. Soon my ordeal is over and the doctor notifies me, "You must go home and stay there for the next two weeks."

A few days later my wife also comes down with the flu-like symptoms. Since I don't want her to go alone I accompany her to the hospital where once again we are subjected to the same behaviour, we feel as if we have the plague.

Arriving back home I spend my days in bed curled up in front of the television. Time flows slowly like wet cement. After two weeks of self-imprisonment, we are both feeling better and we return to our places of work. Our co-workers are unnerved by our presence and keep their distance from us.

Now a few months later I can see the funny side of events, with everyone running for their lives wherever we went, but at the time it felt dreadful. Since the coronavirus has become an epidemic the national health in Israel has become much more efficient. They send paramedics in protective clothing to visit prospective corona victims in their homes to take saliva and blood tests. In the meantime, the world waits in anticipation for a vaccination to be discovered.

Walking and Talking

Jim Bates

For years I've taken a walk every morning in our small town. There's a trail along a roadway near where I live and I love getting out and enjoying a bit of fresh air, especially now when winter is losing its icy grip and springtime is fast approaching. In the past few weeks the snow has melted away completely and the lakes have lost their covering of ice and opened up. It's delightful being outside. I even heard a song sparrow singing the other day.

Most days I'd see only a handful of people. We'd rarely greet, preferring, instead, to pass on by with our heads down, ignoring each other and carrying our special solitude deep inside. Then Covid-19 reared its ugly head: people getting sick, people dying, not enough medical supplies to go around and a president who had no empathy for the situation whatsoever. Then came lockdown. Traffic dwindled to the bare minimum, people were warned to stay inside, and, if they did go out, to maintain a safe social distance. Life went on but in a different way as we all learned to adjust.

These days I still go for my walk, but I've noticed something has changed: more people are out walking than ever before. And, as opposed to the rather perfunctory nod like in the past, they are giving out a friendly wave, as if to say, *We're all in this together. Take care*. (While maintaining a respectable social distance, of course.) It's nice to see. Also, people are spending more time in their yards, having parked their cars for the foreseeable future. The truth of the matter is that folks are taking it upon themselves to get used to being at home. Life has slowed down and become more family orientated. Distance learning is in place now for the kids as parents become teachers.

Today, while walking by my neighbor's house, she looked up from raking her lawn, brushed a wisp of hair from her forehead and said, being friendly, "We're taking a recess. Thank goodness the weather's nice so the kids can play outside."

She pointed. Her young boy and girl were playing on a front yard swing set. I waved to them and they waved back. I turned to my neighbor, "So, how are you doing?" I asked, keeping six feet away.

"Good," she said. "It's hard. An adjustment. I miss my job, but the kids love having me home."

"That sounds like a good thing," I said.

She smiled, "Yeah. It is."

We said good bye and I continued my walk. A flock of robins up ahead fluttered away from a puddle of water they'd been drinking from. A mother and father and their three kids rode by on their bikes. They smiled and waved. I waved back, thinking, maybe we'll all be better neighbors to each other when all this is over. Better human beings.

When I got home I washed my hands and then called my son and two grandchildren. I used to see them every week but that was before the pandemic. I missed them and it was wonderful to hear their voices. We talked for a while until the kids had to leave. "We love you," they said.

"I love you, too," I told them, not wanting them to go.

And, at that very moment, in spite of all the horror and uncertainly of the future, just the sound of my loved ones' voices and knowing they were well and safe, made everything all right.

"I'll call you every day," I told my son.

"That'll be good, Dad," he said. "I'd like that." He paused. "Well, good bye."

"Good bye."

I sat and stared into space, thinking, before deciding what to do: I'd make a pact with myself. I would stay positive because tomorrow was another day. And another walk. More people to greet. And now, a special phone call to make.

Yes, that was as good a way as I could think of to get through this. I smiled, already looking forward to tomorrow. Then I sealed my pact with love.

Empathy Works

Susan A Eames

My life was compartmentalised into three phases:
Life Before the Virus
Life During the Virus
Life After the Virus.
During phase two, I fled the anarchy and found refuge in a remote village.
The locals showed me how to survive, how to share. Who said Communism was evil?
Food was harvested and left for everyone to help themselves. We looked after each other.
Sometimes it was hard.
In Life After the Virus, I'm still here. The outside world remains a dangerous place. They don't know how to share. They still don't understand that empathy works better than anarchy.

COVID – Taste

Amanda Jones

Wiping, hand wash, aware,
A cough, a sneeze, a stare.
This is my every day,
Keeping germs at bay.

A simple cold on the chest
Keeps my hands at best,
Wiped, washed, clean,
Behind a normal scene.

Then Covid-19 came,
Suddenly all to blame.
Hygiene up, isolating
My everyday Covid rating.

Shielding for twelve weeks flat,
Who would ever think that
A simple cold could also do
What Covid-19 threatens to.

I peer from my doorway
And glimpse a look at the day
Relishing my view and moment
Just as every day is meant.

Covid-19 has given all
A chance to see things small.
The business has stopped
And money has been cropped.

Glance at how I risk each day
In socialising, work and play
Each time a germ leaves you
I could end up
Like
Covid-19 may
Treat
You.

The Gathering

Peter Astle

"You can't be serious," Jane said. "You'll be thrown in jail."

Paul shrugged. "We might as well be in jail. Besides, this is important. It's just one night."

"It's martial law," Jane reminded him. "Public gatherings are illegal."

"It's a private gathering. Everyone will be wearing masks and gloves."

Jane clattered dinner plates in the sink. Melody, their skinny tabby cat, leapt off the table and curled by her feet. "Are you out of your mind? Seriously, Paul. Thousands of deaths every day, police drones monitoring the streets. We can't even go food shopping now."

That was true. All food retailers were now officially closed to the public. Public places had been shut down indefinitely. Home deliveries were mandatory. Full lockdown was now in force across the globe. The virus had spread so fast, Armageddon was the word on everyone's lips. And Paul Swain was climbing the walls.

After the second month of lockdown, when the global death toll reached unimaginable numbers, politicians across the world had no other choice but to enforce total self-isolation. The motorcyclists who left essential food supplies on doorsteps across the country wore sanitised gloves, and surgical masks behind their helmets. They rarely spoke to the customers they delivered to.

Social media was clogged with messages of doom. Many people sought sanctuary in private online groups – religious and otherwise – that offered some light at the end of the tunnel. Paul Swain, landlord of the Bull's Head in Buxton, had developed one such group. He called it 'The Gathering'. All thirty-six private members were former customers of the Derbyshire pub, which had been forced to close three months ago due to the worldwide pandemic. Many customers were elderly, completely isolated, scared, desperate for human contact. The online group provided some company, discussion and distraction, but it wasn't enough. People needed people.

"I've contacted everyone in the group," Paul said. "None of them have the symptoms."

Jane rattled cutlery in the sink. "If there's a chance that even *one* of them has the virus, it's not a chance worth taking. I'm a key worker, Paul. This afternoon I had to turn away Vera Howard from intensive care. Maddie Howard's sister, for crying out loud. This thing has to stop."

Paul knew all about Maddie Howard. Just about everyone in the country did. Paul sipped his mug of tea. "It's a bit late for that now. They'll all be coming tonight, around eight o'clock."

Jane dropped a Denby cereal dish. It smashed on the stone floor tiles next to the sink. Melody shot across the kitchen as though a bomb had exploded.

By nine o'clock the beer was flowing at the Bull's Head. Behind the bar, Paul grinned as he served drinks to customers he'd not seen in three months. Everyone wore the agreed surgical gloves and masks, pulling up the mask to take a drink. Blackout curtains hung at each window, a precaution someone in the private group had suggested to thwart the police observation drones. Jane flatly refused to attend. Right now, she was upstairs on the office computer, deleting every thread from 'The Gathering' homepage.

Reverend Frank Pendleton came across to the bar, leaned towards Paul and whispered through his mask, "Maddie's outside."

Paul pulled the vicar to one side. "She can't be."

"She called the neighbourhood phone line. We've been offering welfare services, remember?"

Paul nodded. The health authorities and the military were so overstretched, the clergy had been called upon by the government to offer personal pastoral support to the over-seventies. Many had no internet access, no means of socialising other than the phone. Frank Pendleton was part of the government-funded initiative, Neighbourhood Welfare, designed to help alleviate the psychological effects of complete isolation. He and two dozen volunteers spent up to six hours a day and night talking to the elderly across Derbyshire, keeping them informed, keeping them safe, keeping them company.

"How the hell did Maddie find out about this?"

"It wasn't me who took the call. Loose lips and all that. I've no idea. But she's in the car park right now, arms folded across her chest. Collared me a few minutes ago as I was coming in. She wants to talk to your wife."

Paul blew out his cheeks. "Jane mentioned something about her sister, Vera. Did she say what it was about?"

"Only that she'd call the police if Jane won't speak to her."

Paul snatched up the entrance hatch at the end of the bar. "Mind helping out behind here?"

Frank gave a salute and slipped behind the bar.

Customers patted Paul on the back with gloved hands as he made his way towards the stairs in the corridor. He'd not done a headcount, but he was pretty sure that all thirty-six members had made it tonight. Someone amongst this group had alerted Maddie to the gathering, but there was no time to worry about that now. He ran up the stairs, two at a time. Jane was in the office hammering away at the computer keyboard, her back towards him.

"Maddie's outside," he said. "She wants to talk to you."

Jane continued to type. "I'm shutting down your little group."

"She says she's going to call the police if you don't see her."

Jane turned to look at him. In twenty years of marriage he'd seen her angry, but nothing like this. Written on her face was pure fury, maybe even a touch of disgust. "The world is falling apart and *you* – against all medical advice – decide to throw a party."

"It's not a party. It's a private gathering. We're all masked and protected."

"It's against the law. You could be arrested. Fined heavily. We're in total lockdown, Paul. Social distancing is law. What were you thinking of?"

"The community, actually," Paul said. "The older people. They're all going stir crazy out there on their own."

"Better to be stir crazy than to pass the virus on."

Paul knew it was pointless arguing with his wife on this one. As an intensive care unit worker, Jane was part of the 'Keep Your Distance' campaign from the outset.

"If you don't speak with her, she'll call the police. Do we need that?"

"I can't speak to her. She's suing the hospital. We've been told to have no contact with her whatsoever. You know the trouble she's caused."

Paul knew. It had made national headlines. Local hero Maddie Howard was taking the hospital to court for age discrimination – and according to her lawyers, she would win.

Two months ago, when the virus hit its first peak, the emergency services were stretched beyond their limits. Senior doctors had to make tough decisions as to who and who not to treat in intensive care. It was no first come first served situation.

Various factors were taken into consideration when it came to allocating intensive care unit beds, and age was one of them. Maddie's lawyers obtained a leaked bed-allocation document that showed a system whereby patients were scored. In a nutshell, the older the patient, the lower the overall score, and the less likely they'd be treated. What it meant in reality was that if two people presented exactly the same symptoms – say an eighty-year-old and a thirty-year-old – the younger patient would get the ICU bed. Younger people recovered more quickly, thus freeing up the bed for others patients. Maddie was eighty-three when she called the hospital with a fever. She was turned away, even though there were beds. The beds went to younger, more 'efficient' patients. The same source at the hospital who leaked the bed-allocation document to the media also provided Maddie with this nugget of information.

Ill as she was, Maddie went straight to the press. The story caused a media storm in the tabloids and serious discussion in the broadsheets. Terms like 'institutionalist ageism', 'playing God', and 'utilitarianism' were debated in the House of Commons. The hospital released a brief statement – they had little choice given the public outcry and the existence of the leaked bed-allocation document –

which said although they could not comment on individual cases, in a state of national emergency, it had 'Now become necessary to establish an age limit for access to intensive care'.

This fanned the flames even further. When Maddie's story went viral, the Prime Minister was forced to make a statement outside Number 10. He admitted the National Health Service was currently overstretched but measures were being implemented to safeguard the public: retired doctors and nurses were to return to work, there was government funding for more intensive care units across the country, the majority of workers' wages would be paid by the government in this time of crisis, and new initiatives like Neighbourhood Welfare – which specifically provided support to the elderly – were being rolled out across the country.

At no point did he mention Maddie Howard.

He repeated the mantra about washing hands and even managed a brief smile after his now familiar parting shot – "Stay indoors, stay informed, stay safe" – before hotfooting it back through the famous black door.

That was just the start of it.

Fortunately, Maddie Howard recovered. Unfortunately, she became more irascible. Through social media she built a huge following amongst the elderly across the UK as the world slid towards total lockdown. In television and radio interviews Maddie stated, with some eloquence, that she was seeking no financial compensation from the hospital, nor from the government. She spoke with the authority of the Belper headmistress she once was. What she sought was justice for the elderly, equality of medical care for a generation of equal importance. In these turbulent times, the most vulnerable people in society were being sent home to die. Someone had to do something.

"She called Neighbourhood Welfare," said Paul. "Her sister's ill."

"I know. I was the one who had to turn her away this afternoon, remember?"

"Which might be the reason why she wants to speak with you."

"I don't make the rules, Paul."

“Please speak to her. I’ll come with you.”

Jane opened the drawer under the computer desk and pulled out a fresh surgical mask and a pair of thin protective gloves. “I’ll speak to her if you promise to send everyone home. This gathering has to stop.”

Paul held up two gloved palms. “Let’s see what she wants.”

From the very start of total lockdown people fell into two camps: those who stuck to the rules, and those who did not.

Working in an intensive care unit, Jane had no choice other than to toe the line. Working in the pub industry, Paul did not. Sure, he washed his hands, wore surgical gloves and masks when they became compulsory, but social distancing was not so easy. Many of his regular customers were old. The pub was their haven, their social playground, their sanctuary. Paul understood the logic behind social distancing, but human contact was essential. Lockdown may have slowed down the spread of the virus, but total isolation for many people was a living nightmare. For Paul, the one-off gathering was about restoring what was before. Even if just for one night.

Maddie Howard stood in the carpark wearing standard surgical gloves and mask, arms crossed against her chest, just as Frank Pendleton had described. She stood no more than five feet tall but somehow managed to look formidable despite wearing a pink cardigan and matching tracksuit bottoms. The Champion for the Elderly stood before them, defiant, unashamed, and angry as hell.

“I’m sorry about Vera,” Jane said, folding her own arms to mirror Maddie’s. “I had no choice.”

Paul stayed back, six feet behind his wife, close to the stone steps at the entrance of the pub.

“I’ve not come to argue,” Maddie said. “I’ve come to deliver a message to my friends.”

Jane said nothing.

“You want to come inside?” Paul asked.

“Yes. I’ve got something to tell you all.”

Jane took a step closer. "The party's over, Maddie. It never should have happened in the first place. We're sending everyone home."

"Let me speak to them first."

"It's impossible. I've been told to have no contact with you."

"I'm dropping the court case," Maddie said. "Things have changed."

Once again, Jane was lost for words.

"If you want to come into the pub, that's fine by me," Paul said.

"What things have changed?" Jane asked.

"I'll explain. But I need to do this face to face."

Paul gathered everyone into the lounge for the speech. It could just about take thirty-six people.

Gloved and masked and all holding drinks, they crammed into the small space, shoulder to shoulder, hushed in anticipation. Muted handclapping came the moment Maddie walked into the room, the surgical gloves dampening the sound of the applause. For many in this room, Maddie Howard, was their hero, the Champion of the Elderly, a local ex-headteacher turned celebrity who had stood up to the Prime Minister in the glare of the media and at the height of a global crisis. Paul moved a table in the corner of the lounge to give her a spot to stand. Maddie took it and faced the crowd. She looked so small and ordinary in her pink cardigan and tracksuit bottoms, but her expression radiated confidence, chin held high, eyes falling on each member of the gathering.

"I'm here to tell you something important," she began. "I spoke with a junior health minister today, from the government."

Paul and Jane exchanged a glance as gasps and whispers rippled through the crowd.

"As many of you know," she continued, "I was ill last month, like so many others. I managed to pull through at home, but only just. I was turned away from hospital even though there were ICU beds. I was turned away because of my age."

She let that one hang in the air for a full five seconds. No one spoke, but there were plenty of glances across the room.

"The same thing happened to my sister, Vera, today. She's seventy-seven – six years younger than me. Merely a child."

Nervous laughter came from somewhere near the back of the lounge. Jane stepped close to Paul, squeezed his hand.

"Vera's staying with me for now. Hopefully that will change. I can only nurse her best as I can, as safe as I can for the foreseeable future. I don't have access to ventilators or any other intensive care equipment at home. I don't even have Alexa."

Another murmur of laughter from the back.

"People compare this pandemic to the war years." Maddie shook her head. "It's nothing like that. Those days we dug for victory, together. We worked together, fought together, survived together. We pulled together. This *thing*, this virus, is driving us apart, separating us, scaring us half-way to death." She looked across to Paul. "I understand your need for this gathering, Paul. But this has to stop."

Paul was about to protest when Jane gave his arm a firm tug.

"We can stick together through this online. We can call one another on the phone. We cannot meet in groups. My sister would not be infected today had I not ignored the advice and visited her."

"But we're protected," someone shouted from the crowd, waving a gloved hand.

"Not enough," Maddie said. "As I say, I spoke with an MP this afternoon. Angela Fox, junior health minister. Mainly about the age discrimination case, but also about the virus itself. It's airborne but also lives on surfaces. Masks and gloves help, but they're not enough. People touch their faces all the time. How many times have you pulled up your mask to have a drink tonight? How many surfaces have you touched tonight with those latex gloves?"

Paul went to scratch an itch on his neck. Changed his mind.

"But that's not why I've come tonight."

Absolute silence.

"I've come to tell you there will be new hospital guidelines in place as from tomorrow. Angela Fox is on side – she's pretty high up in the government food chain. She thanked me for highlighting the issues faced by the over-seventies. The Prime Minister will be making an announcement tomorrow morning outside Number Ten."

Frank Pendleton leaned over the bar. "So, you're dropping the discrimination case?"

Jane clenched Paul's hand.

"Yes. Angela Fox told me the new government guidelines would legally prevent any hospital discriminating on the grounds of age. Bed-allocations in intensive care units will be open to all, where available. ICU tick-lists will no longer exist. Not much point in going through the courts when the rules have changed. She promised to do all that she could to find a bed for Vera. And I'd like to say—"

"And you believe the words of a politician?" someone from the crowd interrupted.

Maddie composed herself, straightened her mask. "Yes, I do. Angela was genuinely shocked. Her own mother is in her late eighties, with breathing problems. She had no idea these tick-lists existed. Nor did the government."

"Until the leak," Frank said from across the bar.

"Until there was proof," Maddie corrected. "There was always speculation in the media about age discrimination, plenty of anecdotes, but nothing tangible. Tough decisions had to be made by senior doctors and age was rumoured to be a factor. There was never any proof. Not until the leaked bed-allocation document. That changed everything."

"Do we know who leaked it?" Frank asked.

Maddie offered a fleeting glance towards Paul and Jane before returning to the crowd. "We have no idea. But what I'd like to say was thank you. Thank you to whoever it was."

Jane lowered her head. Paul gently squeezed her hand.

"Now," Maddie said in her best headmistress's voice. "It's time to go home."

Sleep, Perfect Sleep!

Phyllis J Burton

I didn't sleep very well last night. Recently, I've been amazed at how quickly I've managed to get to sleep, but fear of catching the coronavirus suddenly caught up with me. My husband was lying beside me and snoring loudly. How can he be so relaxed I asked myself? I remember looking at the clock at about midnight, then again about half an hour later. This continued until about 3 am and I could stand it no longer. I climbed reluctantly out of my really comfortably warm bed and walked around the bedroom for a while. The moon was trying valiantly to light up my life, but some annoying clouds drifted over and took it away again. How many people were just looking at the moon, and desperately hoping that it would shine on a world free from the Covid-19 virus, as everyone is now calling this abominable destroyer of human life. Wouldn't it be wonderful to switch on the television and be told that we had nothing more to worry about?

Has anyone mentioned about climate change: has this been forgotten? But then climate change was something that could happen in years to come, wasn't it? But Covid-19 is here, and it is staring us all in the face and terrifying the life out of us.

The virus is not like some bogey-man who only needs to frighten the life out of you. Nor is it someone who breaks into your house to steal something that you treasure. You can't see the virus, you can't smell it, but it attacks you nevertheless. I am washing my hands so much that they are now feeling sore. I started off by singing HAPPY BIRTHDAY TO YOU twice in exactly twenty seconds, but now I count up to about twenty or thirty seconds in my head. You can possibly gather that I'm a bit of a worrier: I worry about most things, and let's face it, we have a lot to be worried about nowadays, and food is at the top of the list. My husband and I, being of a certain age, have been encouraged to stay indoors and let other people bring our groceries etc. to our house. This is a wonderful service, but once it has been delivered, I spend an enormous amount of time washing everything that comes out of the bag… even down to packets of cereal, and individual tomatoes. Am I taking things a little too far you may ask? But secretly, are you doing this yourselves, if not then perhaps you should?

There are some wonderful people about: selfless people who look after us when we become ill, and then become ill themselves. Every day, we hear about NHS workers who are succumbing to this dreadful disease while helping others. Not only health workers either: there are thousands of people who are helping us to stay safe. They come from every kind of job: the police, lorry drivers, the armed forces, retired people who give up their retirement to resume their old jobs. Sometimes they become ill themselves. The list is endless. I would like to put on record how grateful we are, (or should be) for their diligence and love. Yes, I mean love: not familial love. Love makes the world go round for the continuation of humanity, because where would we be without such wonderful people. Clap hands every night even if you are sitting in your armchair each evening, and nobody else can hear you. The first time we were asked to clap for the NHS, I stood outside my front door and clapped loudly, but I couldn't hear anyone else doing it, because my neighbours were too far away: but I did it nevertheless. Whoever first thought about this should be applauded.

I am lucky. I don't live in a crowded town or city. I live in the countryside surrounded by trees, birds and animals. I can walk in the woods and every day watch as the bluebells come out of the soil and start to bend their heads in a beautiful blue haze.

How long this virus will be with us, is an unanswerable question. We have to believe that it will be defeated and this beautiful world can eventually (and I mean the word 'eventually') return to normal. But what is normal?

I can only hope that once Covid-19 has lost its power to kill, everyone in the world will forget about domination, and can live their lives in peace.

A forlorn hope? I hope not… but our future really does depend on it.

Good health and good luck to everyone, and whatever you do**… DO GET A GOOD NIGHT'S SLEEP.**

Currents

Neta Shlain

I used to read horoscopes at night before falling asleep;
now I browse Coronavirus updates.
Coronavirus update UK—
Unmistakable white-haired head
is the first thing I see, moving on to the number of cases
for today. Thousands new, some percentage of those who'd managed,
inevitably seeing the unlucky ones, hundreds in some
cases.
Yesterday went for a walk keeping two metres
apart, thinking how challenging must be to stay
confined with a family
of strangers, say a husband with skirts on the side
or a wife with a beard in the office.
Now facing that which was avoided for years
quite manageably. In challenging times as these, nervous
tectonic plates shift. The minds of many
will bend into artful lanes, others to others,
with truthful lava outbursts.

Alone

Helen O'Neill

'Stay Inside.' The instruction was clear. But what the letter didn't do was explain why or for how long, so I discarded it with the other junk mail and reached across the kitchen island to pour a large glass of Malbec. It had been a long day in the office and I wriggled my grateful toes as I freed them from their stiletto confines. The microwave purred in the background. Our cleaner was always chastising me for wasting the expansive kitchen and I'm sure that part of the reason she left food for me at the end of her shift, was to enjoy the pleasure of cooking in it. It was an arrangement that suited us both and when David was travelling for business, I was particularly grateful. I savoured the relaxing warmth of my first mouthful of wine and booted up the laptop; America would be waking up soon.

Finally satisfied that the day's work was complete, I headed to the living room and sank into the leather sofa, flicking on the news. The images were compiled from clips recorded on people's phones, hastily edited together to provide a visual backdrop to a message that elaborated on the letter I'd so easily ignored. The words were repeated: 'Stay inside, lock the doors and the quarantine evaluation team will be with you shortly.'

People were fleeing in panic and the army was struggling to keep control. There were burning buildings and looting. Roads were gridlocked and fights were breaking out on the streets. The images were terrifying. It made it real. It made me comply.

I reached for my mobile and swiped for social media, only to find that it wouldn't connect. I tried calling David and, in the process, confirmed that the phone lines were down too. I considered my choices and with the news still pumping out images of mayhem, I did as I'd been instructed and calmly packed a bag of essentials, leaving it by the front door that I checked to make sure it was secure. I poured the last of the wine and watched the images increase in intensity until my eyes closed and I slipped into sleep. I didn't notice when the television and all the lights in the house went off.

A week is a long time to be in a house on your own. I'm reluctant to leave the sanctuary of the master suite, but as the low, angry growl of my stomach contracting becomes more persistent, I sit up and look over instinctively at the clock, its once familiar red digits still truant. I'm fully clothed under the Egyptian cotton spread, my jeans soft from days of wear and my sweater hood pulled up over lank hair. My movements echo in the unnatural silence as I reluctantly pull the covers aside and stand, finding that I am quite terrified of going downstairs; as if the monsters are down there waiting for me.

In the stairwell I no longer bother trying the light switch for my decent. At the bottom, I catch my toe on the holdall and swear. The door is still locked from the inside with the chain on and the bolt pulled across for protection, but whether it's me being protected from the world or the other way around, I'm not so sure.

In the kitchen, all the cupboard has to offer is a bag of dried pasta and a sorry looking row of tinned food. I choose a can at random. The label worn and the rim an aged orange, and then I search the cutlery draw for an opener to defeat the lid. After a struggle, my efforts are rewarded with bland beans in watery ketchup. I pick up the same fork I've used every day and wiped clean after every meal. It feels unnatural to eat from a tin and not fill the dishwasher when I'm done, but the water stopped running on day two, so reusing a fork is the least of my hygiene worries.

I try the taps anyway and the pipes bang angrily at me. I regret not filling up pans, the bath. I thought they would be here by now. I didn't expect to have to ration food and water. I don't know what I did expect.

The fridge has a strange smell. In the dark, it holds the last bottles of lemonade that will save me from dehydration. I take one and carry it with me to the living room where I sit crossed legged on the rug. I twist the cap and listen to the pathetic sound of carbon escaping. The beans taste metallic as I place them individually into my mouth washing them down with the flat lemonade. I eat slowly, and I wait.

I can't hear anyone in the house next door. David and I used to complain about the children as they rushed up and down the stairs or in circles around each other in the garden. I find I miss it now. As I sit, the semi-dark becomes complete dark, so I light a candle on the mantelpiece and watch as the flame flickers. It's rose scented and casts a comforting glow, but as the candle burns and marks the passing of another day, I know the time for waiting is through. Tomorrow, I'll have to go outside.

I run my finger along the edge of the shelf looking for a street map, collecting dust I hadn't realised was there and wiping it on my jeans. The collection of books is limited to celebrity chefs and assorted titles of unwanted gifts. We preferred digital information but I'm sure I had an old map somewhere, one of those items that we just hadn't got around to throwing away.

When I find it, its pages are difficult to navigate. I've become used to electronic applications that only require the slightest intervention. I'm looking for inspiration, for a sign telling me where will be safe, and as my eyes scan the pages it's the public buildings that seem the most sensible choice.

I'm feeling more optimistic than I have in days; decision and activity have reinvigorated me. Emptying out the contents of the holdall, I ridicule my earlier choices and kick the pile to the side. I line the bottom of the bag with the remaining cans and tuck the opener into the side pocket. I pack extra layers of clothes, warm sensible ones rather than smart impractical ones. I leave the electronic devices on the floor next to my make-up bag and replace them with the map and the last of the candles along with a box of matches. I pause and pick up the frame holding a picture of David and I on holiday last year and the realisation strikes me that I may never see him again. I remove the frame and add the picture to the bag; some things are too valuable to leave behind.

If I'm going outside, I should get some rest. I tell myself I will sleep one last time in my own bed, then, in the morning, I'll change my clothes and make myself as presentable as possible. I'd hate to be turned away from salvation. My mind is racing with all the possibilities tomorrow might bring, playing out scenarios, both good and bad. I don't sleep well. As I drift in and out of consciousness my mind wanders to places I don't want to be.

I dream that morning has arrived and I have my hand on the door as I work up the courage to open it when there is a loud knock from the other side. I fumble with the lock and pull the door open. There is a limousine waiting at the bottom of the driveway, so I pick up my bag and make my way towards it. I climb inside and David hands me a china cup filled with the sweetest tea I've ever tasted. The radio is playing a song I don't recognise, but I find myself tapping my fingers to the calming beat.

Sitting up with the stark realisation that the taping is not in the dream, but coming from the window, my body floods with adrenalin and I rush over to pull back the drapes, then immediately cower from the bright light that rushes into the room. My hands shield my eyes and I peer through my fingers, not sure if I want to see what's on the other side. There is a drone hovering behind the glass and its electronic eye is scanning me. I take the stairs in pairs, not wanting whoever sent the drone to miss me and forgetting the holdall I'd so carefully prepared, I fall onto the driveway.

Above the house is a plastic dome. The drone hovers above my head and showers me with a fine mist that smells of disinfectant and contrasts with the stale air. It lowers to face me and I see my reflection, barely recognisable in its lens, then there is a flash and it flies away leaving me in solitude once more.

I walk across the brown lawn to the place where the dome touches the floor and I cup my hands to its translucent covering. I can make out the shapes of vehicles and what I think must be people on the other side, but it's like trying to watch a film without my glasses on. I walk the circumference of the dome looking for a way out, for my rescue. When I reach the driveway, I see an envelope on the ground and kneeling on the cold concrete I slip my finger under its seal. It contains printed commands: 'Stay inside. Successful quarantine confirmed. Evacuation imminent.' And beneath the formal text a hand-written sentence:

Stay safe, love David.

And I know I am no longer alone.

A Visit to the Pharmacy

Misha Herwin

The sky is a sharp blue and there is a bite to the air. The April sun throws shadows onto the pavement and, after the silence of our street, the sound of the few cars going up the hill is painfully loud. Arriving at the pharmacy, I join the queue. Without being told we are standing two metres apart. We are all women. The one in front of me looks nervous. Her gaze flits from her phone to the pharmacy door. Behind me the others keep their heads bowed over their screens. Not daring to look up they encapsulate themselves in a familiar bubble. No one speaks.

Only a few weeks ago, there would have been chat and banter, complaints about how long we must wait, how long it took to get an appointment at the doctor's. Now there is nothing.

A woman with a stick comes towards us. Black hair, aged skin, a slash of red lipstick, she peers at the notice on the pharmacy door. "Only two people at time."

Will she try to jump the queue? Does it matter if she does? There is time enough for me to wait.

The door opens. A woman comes out, another goes in. Time stretches. The black-haired woman shakes her head and moves slowly away. Slightly off balance she keeps closer than she should and the queue shrinks closer to the buildings to give her space. Then she is gone, away down the hill.

Second in line, my turn comes. Yellow and black tape, like that used at a crime scene, separates me from the desk. The pharmacist wears a mask and gloves. I state my name. He goes into the back of the shop and comes out with my husband's prescription. There is no need to sign. The pen I was so careful to bring will be returned to its pot uncontaminated.

Carrying the paper bag home, I bypass other pedestrians. We keep our eyes down. There is to be no contact, not even a smile.

Fear of staying in, of being confined within the walls of our homes, has turned into fear of going out. Every person out there is a possible carrier, or spreader of the virus. The world is full of the unseen enemy and to defeat it we must behave in this alien and inhuman way.

Coming home, I feel safe again. I take off my gloves, wash my hands and settle down at the computer. Here I enter a place of kindness and concern. People ask each other how they are coping, post encouraging memes, find ways of distracting each other. Friends ring, neighbours offer help. We can't touch, we can't talk face to face, but we are caring for and supporting each other.

Digitally, we don't avoid eye-contact. The next time I go out, I will not forget to smile and nod, or wave hello. I will treat the people I pass as fellow human beings and hopefully that will brighten their day and mine.

Changing the Environment

Val Owen

"We have got to do something," said the puffin. "They have warmed the sea and we have lost our food."

The penguin turned to the polar bear. "We may be poles apart but we are both losing our ice."

"Yes," snorted the Scottish wildcat, "they have killed most of us and now all we can do is breed with their domesticated things."

"Our habitat and food is going," cooed the turtle dove.

"We have been pushed to a Welsh island and some areas of Scotland by their meddling," complained the red squirrel.

"They have filled our oceans with plastic," sang the whales.

"Something has got to be done," was the chorus from the capercailles, water voles, dormice and hedgehogs.

"Their numbers and activities need reducing," hooted the owl.

"But how?" was the question from the assembly.

"I have an idea," was the squeak from a bat, but the comment was pitched too high for many of the other creatures to catch.

The cricket offered to relay the bat's comments for those who could not hear. Meanwhile a sniggering jackal at the back of the crowd suggested to a giggling chipmunk that the bat would turn the world upside down so that humans would fall off.

"I may be small," continued the bat, "but I am able to resist diseases, illnesses which would kill humans."

By now all the animals were listening and as the bat paused the elephant asked how this illness could infect humans. The bat explained it was a virus which needed to be passed to humans and to do that there would have to be an animal which would make a noble sacrifice. At this point the lion edged forward.

"No, not you," squeaked the bat and he looked down at the pangolin. The pangolin moved its scaly tail in understanding and acceptance of what would be necessary.

And, dear reader, we all know the outcome of the actions of the bat and the pangolin.

Good Healing Earth

Angela Armstrong

Like running water, energy will flow once more.
In trickles and torrents,
through streets like veins,
in the crevices of homes
and within the chasms of society,
Through countryside lanes
and in people's thoughts and minds.
It will pulse, like a heartbeat
and will drum to raise spirits, compassion and hope.

Existence will come through time and great vision,
through absolute passion
generous dedication,
with fortitude
and whatever else it takes…
to banish and expel all that is unblessed, unholy, uncharitable
about this malevolent spectre in secret and deadly form!

For better, for worse in this oneness, take your pick wisely
I choose 'for better' and hope for Earths healing
Like an 80's pop slogan, inviting a decision
I choose my life… to live
and I intend to!
I'll move onwards to
new horizons, that will stretch my mind's eye forward
and beyond this sickening ravage and desolation.
Destiny is within us and not as a remote concept
but in deeds
and in actions
and in unselfish love.

All this, when we take note,
will be like the therapeutic clarity of a starlit sky
To wish upon,
to provide space to rethink our ways and doings.
For reflection and thoughts
and to be resilient and sometimes silent in questioning.
Who or what's will has caused this abomination of souls and hearts
and insulted mankind itself?
Is it a test of mortal values and ethics, to teach us a lesson of
Biblical proportion?

In unity, let us make way together
And answer the call for all to respond.
To act, to heal,
to dispel like rubbish all that is inhumane,
and to dismiss unkindness to this Earth and its beings.
Let us nurture it better
and give back what's been lost and so maliciously denied.
Live cleaner! Live greener! Live caring! That's what is needed!
Respect all forms of life and the abundance is ours
In Peace and co-existence,
Kindness and gratitude
and in accepting the supremacy of what is natural and wholesome.
And when we can all breathe once more, at liberty, al fresco
Open your mind, your pores to nourish the body and spirit within.

Acknowledge what has changed for history and all time
with the recall and reaping of sins some may have fatefully sown.
But… move on and believe, show faith and remembrance.
Let us heal our good Earth and replenish our consciousness too
with thankfulness,
simplicity,
wisdom and truth.
Inhale life in a better place with all its goodness
to practice and preach.

Then, with simple thought and contemplation
live more once again
through yesterdays,
the present
and the yearning for tomorrows
as we are destined to do in more ways than one.

EARTH ONE LIFE HEALED HAPPY LOVED

The Children's Pain

Ella Etienne-Richards

Dad always came home around the same time, although he had longer shifts now. Yet I still waited, patiently. Mum walked slowly into the living room, put her hands on my shoulder and gently turned me around to face her. Instinctively, I knew what she had to say must be dead serious. Sorry Jeff, Dad's contracted the virus. My worse ever nightmare had come true. Mum reassured me that Dad was young, strong and in the care of the best doctors but she was wrong. I will never forgive Covid-19 for robbing me of my rock, my anchor. Gone Forever.

The Corridors of Power

Russell Lloyd

"You sound nasal."

Her words reached me over the slosh of her marigold hands massaging the washing up. Washing up suited her. It was orderly, neat. You put in the water, added plates and so forth and something cheap and lemony and the results were always the same. It was easy, safe and as predictable as the grey yoga pants and Arran cabled, crew neck thigh-length jumper she inhabited our house with on cosy days inside. Sixty-two and heading for the fag end of life now 'the kids were settled', flatlining to comfort. Me, I was a rebel. I filled dishes with water and left them in the sink for the washing-up fairy. I swilled my hands and then wiped the dirt off on the hand towel.

And now we had this.

I was behind her so she was blind to the stillness, sudden and complete, that fettered my truth.

"It's the spring thing, my asthma, the bloody leaves." Only I knew I was lying.

She laughed in an unfunny way, I didn't. She didn't laugh again. There was a silence neither of us would have felt, before. She didn't mind and the dishes seemed indifferent.

"We'll watch a box set, shall we? We like that." She was right, she would. Me, I was going to sit there; my eyes empty of all they saw, noncommittal noises from unenthusiastic lips and an elsewhere mind. I was going to be thinking about 'symptoms', trying to distinguish what I had read from what I was imagining.

All these memories of things banal and home and life and hope hazed away and in their place the corridor here infiltrated my senses, the torpid humid fug of too many people.

"Are you a Leeds fan?" a woman was saying.

It wasn't a genuine question. So far off I could hardly hear her but I had nearly three days here watching the same stuff, a box set that never did vary. 9am prompt, always three of them, on a mission. I had done the counting. They were looking for twenty and no more, sometimes less. She, the woman, had never got this close to me, never got this far down the corridor before. I didn't know her name but I knew now what she was up to. So did she, and it had stooped her stance, made her face haggard, and put a tremble in her blue hands.

Sometimes she got a response, others not. When she was sure, she nodded to one of the other two and he – or was it she, no one could tell – scanned the wristband and marked a clipboard sheet. The third moved the gurney out from the wall. Two more, safely distant, rustled their scrubs into movement and wheeled it off. They didn't say where but I guessed I knew.

Now she was only two trolleys from me. Her face, the face of God, had the remnants of a life erased – Groucho Marx eyebrows ragged with growth and make-up, impossible to get, and now abandoned. I was next. Hope snared my throat with a fear that stole my words. This was my chance to return home. There would not be another. But I knew I was going to fail. Not because I didn't know the answer to the question but because I just couldn't speak. Not my fault. It was Brian's fault.

Brian's hands were what I had noticed first, hanging from the trolley as he had arrived prostrate, moved into an unmoving queue getting longer, not shorter. Hands and fingers, massive things and a torso to match. After he had rallied, we talked a little and not often. "Can you spare the air?" he would say and, if I could, we spoke trolley to trolley – no social distancing for us. It was his humour in a place where there wasn't enough of anything. He didn't get to say much but it was enough to finish me.

He was, so he told me back then days ago, a twenty-three-year-old plumber with a wife that was terrified and two kids who thought he was God. He didn't mean me any harm, he didn't know he was killing me.

"Hello," she said and ripped me from my thoughts of Brian and his talk. Somehow, I did not know how I had got this extra word from her. Usually, it was just the question, always the question and nothing but the question. I knew what to say but could not say it. She waited, it was my last chance. It was everybody's last chance. If you had the breath to say anything you escaped this line of death to an ICU and a ventilator. I'd watched her signal nineteen times already today and nineteen souls had been wheeled off. But then, next in line, there was me and Brian… a Brian not like me, not old like me, with kids not old and settled like mine, not asthmatic… you get the picture. He should have been doing better but this last twenty-four hours he had struggled, his mouth agape, his voice stolen, and his lungs empty.

"Are you a Leeds fan," she added to her 'Hello'. So I spluttered and coughed and gurgled some breaths and my life away. I don't know if Brian appreciated my pretence. I could never know.

She patted my arm and bustled off. I'd gone from her mind before her hand left my arm. The effort had had been worth it, they discarded me and turned to Brian. The struggle had overwhelmed me… I managed a deep breath and it eased out from under my ribs as if dawdling, no coughing, even the cut-glass agony in my lungs had gone, and my chest subsided. It didn't rise again. You think you can be brave. It's not so. My legs thrashed and my fists thumped but not one of the three looked back at me.

Who could blame them? Who would want to see my blue face, terrored eyes… hadn't these three been seared enough by all they had seen? Immune to suffering, theirs and mine, their decisions had inoculated them.

Through my agony, I could see Brian was talking, overexerting himself. He actually did support Leeds. She gestured and Brian, like some Viking longship, was on his way. Only for a moment, Brian arched his back in spasm.

"He's arresting…" the Clipboard said.

"Quick, get the resuss—" she almost squeaked the words.

"No, you know the protocol," said a boot-faced voice I couldn't see, cold as coal black and bleak, and unrelenting.

With a noise like a bottle uncorked, my ribs heaved up. If anything the pain was even worse but I could hear them.

"But, but…" Her plea hoarse, her professionalism abraded into absence.

"But he's got kids and a wife," I rasped and they turned on me.

"No," said the relentless guy, "we'll take this one."

The coppery smell of cylinder oxygen coated my mouth as the mask pushed into my face.

"No… you don't understand, it's Brian you should—"my voice so muffled through the mask I could hardly hear. I kicked and thumped the gurney rails.

Boot-face didn't look at me as he said to her dejected back, "Good choice, see, plenty of life in this one." A life saved by those losing theirs.

Paradise

Jim Bates

My wife and I were sitting in the living room reading and taking frequents breaks to check our phones to see what the recent news was with Covid-19. It was the beginning of the fourth week of the state-imposed lockdown and it already felt we'd been doing this for a year. We were gearing up for a long haul.

Suddenly Emily looked at me and frowned. I met her gaze. "What?"

"Bad news," she said, grimacing.

It seemed like we were spending every minute of every day hearing about and talking about the pandemic. Bad news was becoming a way of life. "Someone we know have the virus?" I asked, my heart rate speeding up.

"Sort of. John Prine died."

"Damn it," I spat out, "I thought he might make it."

We'd read the week before that he'd been infected. He'd been in poor health recently, but still… he was only seventy-three, my age. I loved him as singer songwriter and was sad to hear he'd passed on.

Emily shook her head. "Me, too." She was quiet for a minute before saying, "He'd been in the ICU for eight days."

"Shit," I said, angry at the circumstances causing his death.

But then a song of his came into my head, *Paradise*, and I mellowed out, suddenly at a loss for words, remembering the first time I'd heard his music. It seemed like it was only yesterday…

The year was 1971. I had returned from Vietnam in January and was working that summer as a dishwasher at Ken's Café on the University of Minnesota campus. I'd just gotten back to the apartment after a ten-hour shift and was sprawled on the couch smoking a joint when Tim walked in.

He held up a shopping bag. "Check this out."

"What have you got?" I took a hit and offered it to him. He

took a deep drag and held it in. "John Prine's first album," he said exhaling and coughing a little. "It just came out."

He put it on the turn table and, given what we were doing at that very moment, we were hooked by the first song, *Illegal Smile*. We listened to the album about ten times that night, smoking and talking, digging the music and the words to his songs. We became immediate fans. So did our other two roommates and it became a pattern that summer: coming home from work, smoking our dope and listening to John Prine. I even figured out the chords to the fifth song on the album, *Paradise,* and Tim and I sang it together sometimes while I played guitar. It was a memorable summer.

But then life got in the way. Early the next year Tim was convicted for resisting the draft and was sent to prison in Missouri. I drove down to visit him a few times but tapered off after I started going to college. We eventually lost touch. I heard later that he'd stayed in Missouri after he was released, met a woman named Sunshine and moved to a commune south of Eugene, Oregon.

I finished college with a degree in education and started teaching science in the Minneapolis school system. A few years later I met Emily while we were both working weekends at the North Country Coop. We married and built a life together, living in an older section of Minneapolis and raising three kids. I taught high school biology and Emily was a stay-at-home mom who also worked as a self-employed seamstress. It was a good life, and we had no reason to think we wouldn't be able to live it out to the end of our days the way nature intended. But it turned out nature had other plans in the name of Covid-19.

That night, after we heard the news about John Prine's death, we both went silent for a while. Emily had listened to his first album with her roommates when she'd gone to college and had wonderful memories of those times, much like me and Tim and our friends. The two of us listened to it when we first started dating, sharing a blossoming love for each other as well as John's music, which became sort of a cornerstone for our relationship.

After a while, Emily got up, crossed the living room and hugged me. "We still have his album around here somewhere?"

That old album had long since bit the dust. "Remember? It was pretty beat up," I told her. "I had to replace it with a CD. It's downstairs."

"Why don't you try and find it?" she said and kissed me again.

I went down to my workroom and rifled through my stash of albums and CDs. It didn't take long to put my hands on what I was looking for and I hurried back upstairs, holding the scratched jewel case out for her to see. "Found it."

Emily's bright smile took away some of my sadness. She still made me happy just by being around her. "Let's have a listen."

"Sure. You bet."

We had a little boom box under an end table in the far corner of the living room. I put the CD in, started it and joined Emily on the couch. We listened all the way through; both of us quiet, lost in our memories of way back then.

When it was over, she ran her fingers through my hair and asked, "Didn't you used to play that song, 'Paradise'?"

I grinned. "Yeah, but not very good."

"Do you think you could you play it now?"

I knew what she was asking. She was asking if we could go back to those earlier years when life was simpler and we were first falling in love and didn't even begin to think about something like a pandemic and the possibility of people we knew dying.

"Sure," I said. "I'll be back in a minute."

I went downstairs and got out my old martin, tuned it and brought it back to her. I played the song while Emily listened and hummed along.

Daddy won't you take me back to Muhlenberg County, down by the Green River where Paradise lay.

I'm sorry my son but you're too late in asking. Mr. Peabody's coal train has hauled it away.

Then I played it again.

"Thanks," she said when I finished. "That was nice."

I went downstairs and put my guitar away. When I came back she was on the phone. "Who are you talking to?" I asked.

She covered the mouthpiece. "Jason." We talked to our kids every day, now that the pandemic was so prevalent.

"Let me talk to him when you're done." Jason was our oldest son.

And she did. In fact, we talked to all three of our kids that night, and our grandchildren, too, giving everyone in our family our love and best wishes for them to be safe and well. It seemed like the right thing to do.

There was a pandemic going on and people were dying. We were all trying to survive. I felt that if John Prine was alive he might have done the same thing, call his family and tell them he loved them, maybe even write a song about it. It might have been a little thing, but it made perfect sense. And coming from him, that song would have helped make things a little less crazy. In fact, I'm sure of it.

When we were doing talking on the phone I went back downstairs and got John's CD, thinking that we might want to listen to it again. I grabbed my guitar too, just in case. This pandemic wasn't going away anytime soon. A little music might help.

Extreme Human Behaviour

Dawn Knox

Recently, people have banded together, forming support groups to offer help and comfort to those in need.

Whilst others defraud and scam the vulnerable.

People in their thousands have volunteered to return to work in the NHS; to do their part.

Whilst others deliberately sabotage.

People stay home to prevent the spread of infection.

Whilst others go out.

The continuum measuring human behaviour has always extended from goodness to wickedness but now at this time of global crisis, I'm wondering if we're pushing the boundaries on both. Some people are reaching higher peaks of absolute selflessness whilst others… are not.

Lockdown

P.A. Westgate

Even though he said it himself, the garden looked lovely. He'd never before been able to devote so much time to it. He peered intently at the main flower bed. Was there a weed over there? No, it was clear. He'd weeded that bed earlier in the week and they didn't grow quite that quickly. Perhaps it was time to cut the grass. He surveyed the pristine lawn, the edges neatly trimmed. He sighed. He'd done that only the other day. The hedges too, although they seemed to grow like wildfire after a little rain and some sun, had been clipped a month and a half ago and scarcely seemed to have changed. It would be the same at the front. No, the gardens would offer no opportunities for at least two weeks. He walked slowly along the neatly raked gravel path past the shed, freshly painted, to the garage. He'd tidied in there ages ago.

Turning, he gazed back at the bungalow. The windows sparkled in the afternoon sun. The frames too, being UPVC and not needing much maintenance anyway, were clean and bright. What had seemed a lot of work had been done in a few days and, beyond a wash every week or so, wouldn't need any serious attention until next year. The render he'd painted in the spring was bright and unmarked in the sun. He'd even put a touch of red paint on the tile flaunching around the chimneys. Like the gardens, the bungalow looked like something out of *Homes and Gardens*. He'd always though those houses to be too good to be true. Now he had one himself.

Inside then, but he knew already that he would find nothing needed to be done. Housework and washing up to date and enough meals in the freezer for the next couple of weeks, so he didn't need to do any proper cooking. He'd even ironed whatever was available, even though he'd hardly needed ironed clothes, not seeing anyone for weeks. Was there anything, he wondered, that he could sort through, re-organise, tidy? He sighed again. No. In the evenings, there being even less than usual worth watching on the TV, he'd systematically gone through wardrobe after cupboard after drawer after bookcase. The spare bedroom was now full of bags and boxes destined either for the charity shops or the rubbish tips as soon as both reopened. He'd even moved some furniture around. Finding, to his surprise, that it could be arranged differently and, yes, the rooms, the lounge in particular, looked better, more spacious. That wasn't something you could do more than once every few years though.

After a week of lockdown, when people got used to the restrictions, they were saying what they could do with all that time, how gardens would get more attention, how they'd learn a language, read all those books, write that novel. Now, he realised, he'd seen that, done that, got the T-shirt. Well, not the T-shirt, no one was delivering anything these days and he hadn't written the novel.

His wandering had taken him into the front garden, smaller than the back, and to the front gate. He leaned over and peered up and down the lane. No one was around, not even the dog walkers. Strange, there were usually some going to or coming from the fields 100 yards further along the lane. Come to think of it, he hadn't seen any for a few days now. Nor the neighbours, although he rarely saw the ones on either side in any case. He looked across at Bob & Betty's house. The 'B&B' house they liked to say. Their windows could do with a clean. Maybe he should offer. They were quite a bit older than him and he was no spring chicken himself. He'd waved to them from his garden, what, a week ago was it? Something like that. Maybe he should go across and knock. He didn't like to. Even stepping back to their gate, which was well over the two-metre "social distance" he would still feel uneasy. Who knew what a safe distance was anyway? He would feel terrible if he passed anything on, especially to those, by any definition, vulnerable. Probably silly, he thought, but he didn't walk across.

He supposed he could go to the shop. He'd last been about ten days ago, but didn't really need anything. He'd succumbed to a little panic buying in the run-up to Brexit and was still well stocked with tinned and frozen things as he'd carried on with normal shopping afterwards. He even had an adequate supply of toilet rolls. Could do with some milk perhaps and eggs and some fruit maybe. The last time things had still been a little scarce. Maybe the predictions of long-term shortages were coming true. He had been lucky in getting the last six eggs and the bag of apples the last time. Yes, perhaps a trip to the shop.

There was still no one around. He wondered how his friends and family were. Not that he had many friends and the family, what was left of the family, was quite distant. In the early months there'd been a regular exchange of telephone calls and emails, the odd postcard even. But as the lockdown lengthened, these had dwindled. The last email from anyone had been, he didn't know, maybe a month ago, two? He couldn't remember the last time the postman had delivered.

So, the shop he decided. It was, what, about 1.00pm now? Maybe he'd better have some lunch first. He could thaw a smoked salmon fillet perhaps. Have it with a tin of mixed bean salad. Yes, that sounded nice. Then maybe he should run the vac around. Had he done that yesterday or the day before? Time enough to go to the shop later.

He found that he was again in the back garden. He peered intently at the main flower bed. Was there a weed over there?

Covid-19 April 2020: Irish Woman in Victory Road, London

Maeve Murphy

I am working on my novella. What better thing to do, when everyone is in lockdown and film making is in lockdown too. My husband is using his extra time cooking us some delicious meals and we are liking our extended *us* time. I am growing some cress too, so how that for is new shoots? And I'm listening to the sirens. There have been so many sirens.

Other than that Victory Road is more quiet but not that affected. We know it was Emmy's eighth birthday recently as we can see all the children's Happy Birthday drawings in the windows further down the street. We know there is great community spirit, we all come outside on a Thursday night to clap and cheer the NHS. It's a beauty of a moment that boosts our morale system for the next week. Our neighbour picks us up fresh vegetables at the Farmer's Market and passes us some rhubarb from her allotment. We've helped her with her internet problems and also the local Buddhist group is chanting for health for all in the community and an end to the threat.

And yet I can hear the sirens, it is quite frequent. I don't want to think about what is happening to the person in the ambulance. The word ventilator evokes panic in me. It reminds me of living in Northern Ireland, as a child during 'The Troubles.' We lived in a 'safe' area, in middle class Belfast. That is until, the incendiary bomb device went off across the road in the ex-Lord Mayor's house and we temporarily had to leave our house. Or the shootings during Mass at the local church – that time we all got trapped inside, while two dead bodies lay outside. So I know that the invisible threat, visible on the news or heard via the sirens, is there and can burst through at any time. I do know everything can suddenly change. I also know the awful getting used to the loss of life. What had me tense throughout my body and in a state of constant fear and anxiety just a couple of weeks ago has become a fact of life. I am more relaxed, less terrorised, I've got used to the death toll every night. My husband's distant cousin in North London part of it.

I pray that the sirens don't get any closer, or arrive in Victory Road, as bombs did in the Second World War. They won't. And this will also be history soon. In the meantime, in the spirit of not being defeated I have the treasure of hope. My novella will be finished. The cress will grow. And maybe my heart and all our hearts which have grown so much will keep growing. Love in the time of coronavirus has been in epidemic proportions. Invisible realms exist in more ways than one.

Covid Inspired Haiku and Dribble

Mari Phillips

Daffodils cheer us
sunshine teases through chill wind
comes the viral spring

The last banana
we shared it yesterday, so
nothing for breakfast!

At the edge of life
gasping from the deep shadows
I may not survive.

Envy…

Friends envied their holidays.

"Where are you going next?" featured in most conversations.

"Don't know, we'll see," their stock reply.

Susan reflected on this as she held Jim's hand. This time it was a short break in Milan.

Jim's hand was icy cold; the ventilator whooshed.

They switched it off.

FaceTime Happy Hour

Amanda Huggins

Instead of down the pub, they meet on the iPad – 7.30 every Saturday.

Lockdown small talk first – Pete: selfish neighbours; June: problems working from home; Evie: supermarket idiots; John: inconsiderate joggers.

Then the general knowledge quiz, plugging the gap once filled by vacuous conversation.

Which sitcom featured the fictional character Audrey fforbes-Hamilton?

No panic attacks, no tears, no existential dread. No one they know has died. Yet. This is happy hour.

There is a pause; Evie says her biggest fear is that things will never get back to normal. June nods. But *her* biggest fear is that they will.

Ation Flu

Greg Duncan

To stop the propagation of this Wuhan infestation
And to avoid the decimation of the whole world's population
The official stipulation is home locked isolation.
The suggested recommendation to alleviate frustration
Is solitary perambulation of just one hour's duration
But with the risk of criminalisation we experience some vexation
At the merest contemplation of such forms of relaxation.
It's with heightened trepidation we leave our accommodation
With the valid justification, without food – there'll be starvation.
There's no need for concentration to make the observation
That media dissemination of partial information
Results in consternation with mental desperation
For without imminent termination of this restrictive regulation
We face economic stagnation and social deprivation.
Yet throughout this devastation we have total appreciation
For the lack of hesitation in providing hospitalisation
For those of our great nation in need of medication.
But I would feel a great elation
If I could make a declaration
That there is no ruination
I've just been suffering hallucination.

One Year's Time

Ray Suchow

My beloved brother… one year gone… how I miss you, how we all miss you… I'm so thankful for the gifts of fifty years of memories, for the blessing of our families enjoying the trip of a lifetime to San Diego two years ago, and for a thousand other memories that only you and I will ever know. May you continue to guide us and be with us as we journey forward into a world none of us could have imagined a year ago.

It hurts… it feels wrong… that our families cannot physically be together to remember and celebrate the mirthful, capricious wonder of you. The wider world of now is starkly different than that of a year ago, yet our day-to-day is eerily the same. Once more we're shaken, confused, unsure of our next steps, and reality does not make sense… but somehow we'll find our way forward again, like we did before, so that in a year's time we'll gather – together at last – by that swift-flowing Rocky Mountain stream you loved so much, where we gave you back to the universe. And we will remember you with long-delayed hugs, words, and tears; all the comforts of family denied to us now… but soon to be ours again, in one year's time.

Alone

Henri Colt

I'm alone in the patient compartment of our rig, separated from my driver, who's also a paramedic. He can only hear me through the thick glass window. The ventilator fan is set on high, just like we were told to do after the World Health Organization declared the coronavirus a pandemic with fatal repercussions. We've been out since six this morning. I just chucked the last disposable gown in our emergency kit, and I've been wearing the same N95 respirator mask for three days now. Three twelve-hour shifts, three days in a row, but I consider myself lucky. Friends of mine just have surgical masks, which we know provide no protection. Funny how some bosses suckered us into thinking they did some good, and besides, they said, what else are we to do?

The sixty-year-old diabetic woman we just picked up is pasty-looking and wheezing. Her daughter claimed it was a bad asthma attack and she was out of inhalers, but when we called it in and said the gal's got fever too, they told us it's probably the virus.

I double check her oxygen mask. Her breathing is getting worse, and she can't talk. I take another blood pressure reading – it's low.

I can't feel a pulse.

"What did the dispatcher say?" I shout to my driver.

"It's a forty-five-minute wait at the ER, and we're still ten miles away!" he yells back to me over his shoulder.

"We're screwed," I mutter under my breath, knowing he can't hear me anyway with the sudden yelp of our siren and the screech of our tires on the road.

"I'm giving her a breathing treatment," I holler. He needs to know what I'm doing.

"That's against regulations, remember? No nebulizers in infected patients. It might spread the virus."

"Well, those were guidelines – we never got a written order.

Besides, I don't know if she's infected, and she sure as hell doesn't have COVID-19 positive tattooed across her forehead."

"You're gonna get us fired."

"Just drive," I say.

I break open the nebulizer bag and prop the woman up on the gurney. For a moment, I think she's looking at me, but then her pupils roll up under her eyelids, and her eyes go white. "Damn, she's coding." I jam my fingers over her carotid and can't feel a beat. A lead from the electrocardiogram monitor falls off. I start chest compressions. The rig lurches forward. I can almost feel my driver leaning on the accelerator.

"Let her go," he shouts.

"I'm not giving up no matter what the boss might say." I tear off my fogged-up goggles. "Maybe it's not the virus, maybe—"

She perks up. She opens her eyes. I reconnect the EKG lead and see a waveform.

She's alive.

We pull up to a special entrance of the emergency department. The doors swing open. A doctor and two nurses wearing hazmat suits start dragging the gurney out of the rig.

"What happened?" the doc says, not taking her eyes off my patient.

"Just an asthma attack," I say. "Nothing more."

"You sure?" she says. I can tell she sees the nebulizer. I can tell she knows. I swallow hard.

"I'm sure." We've got another call. I'll file the paperwork when we get back.

"Stay safe," the doctor says, pointing at my goggles before swinging the vehicle door shut, "and…" but the rest of her words drown in the wail of our siren as we take off.

Shielded

Sally Angell

Shutdown. She can't go out. No one can. Not out out. Only leave your house for essential reasons.

Stay in your boxes. Then everyone will be safe, no infection. She makes toast, sniffs. Is it burny? Loss of smell is a sign. But there's just *stale.* And boxed in. The walls press inwards. Her mind shrinks.

Radio bulletins warn the vulnerable. Online videos pump out lessons: drawing, meditation, how to self-fill teeth, for the stir-crazy. The recliner chair is a fortress, books wedging her in.

She hears her own voice, aloud.

"My name is Alona. And I LOVE social isolation."

Ode to Loo Rolls

Sally Angell

Where have all the loo rolls gone, long time passing?
Where have all the loo rolls gone, long time ago?
Where have all the loo rolls gone?
To panic-buyers every one.
When will they ever learn?
When will they ever learn?

How have all the loo rolls gone, long time passing?
How have all the loo rolls gone, long time ago?
How have all the loo rolls gone?
In Tesco fisty-cuffs at dawn.
Stockpilers stole them all.
Stockpilers stole them all.

Why have all the loo rolls gone, long time passing?
Why have all the loo rolls gone, long time ago?
Why have all the loo rolls gone?
With the food stocks now so low
Just jump in the shower.
Just jump in the shower.

Now that all the loo roll's gone, long time passing
Now that all the loo roll's gone, long time ago,
Plumbers in masks and gowns will come
To unblock all the pages of
The Mirror and The Sun.
The Mirror and The Sun.

Where have all the loo rolls gone, long time passing?
Where have all the loo rolls gone, long time ago?
Dreams of Andrex soft four-ply
Or any brand all in a row.
Gone from shop shelves every one.
Gone from shop shelves every one.

No Escape

Jo Dearden

Helen was sitting in her favourite chair half watching the news on the TV in her sitting room. There seemed to be nothing but more gloom and doom about the virus and now there was a case in the village, which was panicking everyone especially as the whole area had been put into lockdown. Two police cars were permanently parked both ends of the village, making sure no one could leave or come in. The local shop was running out of basic supplies, so online shopping was the only option, but Helen didn't find it easy. She'd tried it once, but it took her about two hours to navigate the virtual aisles and endless lists and then the screen had frozen.

She was idly trying to do her tapestry, which lay on her lap as the telly burbled on in the background. She wasn't very good at sewing, but it gave her something to do during the evenings, since her mother had died. Towards the end, her mother had seriously tested her patience, but now she was gone, the house seemed far too big and cavernous. There were dark spaces and rooms she never used, which made her feel uneasy. Sometimes she heard odd sounds, especially at night, which she couldn't explain. The house was also difficult to keep clean as so many things needed repairing or replacing. But the main problem was loneliness. Somehow Mr Right had never materialised in her life, which she hadn't minded whilst working and also there had been her mother to care for. At least she had Baxter, but he was getting on a bit too. She leant down and stroked his ears.

"What would I do without you, you smelly old thing," she said nuzzling her face against his soft downy head. She felt him tense. He jumped up and started barking. Helen then heard someone at the front door.

"Who is it?" she called from the hallway as Baxter barked furiously.

"It's me, June."

Helen unlocked the door. Baggot shot outside, but as soon as he saw June, he wagged his tail running in circles around her.

"There, Baxter. It's only me."

"Not sure you should come in with this virus about," Helen said retreating slightly from the doorway.

"Oh, not to worry. I was passing, so just came to see if you're okay?"

"Actually, there is something you could do for me as you're good with computers. I need some help ordering food online."

"Yeah, sure. But how can I do that if I can't come in."

Helen opened the door wider and June stepped into the hall. She led her to the study and switched on her computer.

"I'm surprised you can't do this. You having worked in finance," June said.

"Give me a spreadsheet anytime. I suppose I just haven't had to do it before."

"I expect there might be some others in the village who need help too," June said as she made a few clicks with the mouse.

"It might be difficult to do that as we're all supposed to be self-isolating."

Baxter started growling. "Shut up Baxter. Lie down," Helen ordered.

Someone else was knocking on the door. "Oh Cripes, maybe it's the police checking up on us," June said.

"You stay here. I'll see who it is."

It was the vicar. "Hello Phyllis. What can I do for you?"

"Can I come in?"

"Not sure you're supposed to," Helen said.

"Thought I saw June here just now."

"Um, well she's helping me with online shopping."

Helen opened her front door and Phyllis brushed past her, her white dog collar gleaming. She marched into the study.

"What are you doing June? We're supposed to be staying in our homes. You could be arrested for breaking the curfew."

"Well, I might ask you the same thing vicar? Don't want you infecting your flock now do we?" June laughed.

“Hmm. It’s not easy is it for those like us who live alone?”

“Would you both like a drink or cup of tea or something?” Helen asked them.

“Oh, why not. Whisky would be lovely. We’re going to die of something in the end,” Phyllis said.

Helen went into the kitchen to get the whisky.

“I found these old glasses, which haven’t been used for years, so hopefully they won’t have any germs on them,” she said as she came back into the study.

“Good thinking,” Phyllis said as she poured a glass of whisky and helped herself to one of the chocolate biscuits that Helen had put on a pretty plate.

“Think we have another case now. It’s all getting rather worrying, especially as our nearest hospital is about forty-five minutes from here,” she said munching the biscuit.

“What about your cows? Could the milk get infected?” Helen asked June.

“I dunno. I suppose it might be possible if this virus mutates.”

“Actually, the main reason I dropped by was to ask you something Helen. I’m just wondering if this big house of yours might be used as a hospital if the village needed it?” Phyllis said, pouring herself another glass of whisky.

“Well… um maybe, but it would need a lot doing to it.”

“We’d all help. It would make us feel useful instead of being stuck at home.”

A flashing blue light flickers through the thin curtains, followed by more loud knocking. Baxter starts barking again.

A voice calls through the letterbox. “Police. Open up.”

“I’ll speak to him,” Phyllis said staggering towards the front door holding her glass of whisky.

“Oh, sorry I didn’t realise it was you here, Vicar. We heard there was a party going on.”

“Nonsense,” she said taking a slurp of her whisky. “Don’t know where you got that idea from.”

The Neighbourhood Botch Scheme

Janet Howson

A week after Flight Lieutenant Alfred Richards retired, he set up a Neighbourhood Watch Scheme. This had been prompted by some 'brainless yobos', as he liked to call them, stealing his potted Boxus Bushes from either side of his front door. He had taken a long time choosing them and then waiting for their delivery.

This was twenty years ago but the announcement of the lockdown brought about by the Covid-19 pandemic, was a call to arms. He appointed himself as a self-styled overseer of his neighbours' coherence to the rules listed by the government. He would be there to remind, encourage and advise. He set up a WhatsApp group using the mobile numbers he had accumulated over the years. Whenever a new neighbour arrived on the road, he would immediately introduce himself and include them, willingly or unwillingly, on his Neighbourhood Watch Scheme. He had given up hosting meetings as everyone seemed too busy to attend or were on cruises, safaris or babysitting. He had never married or fathered children, he realised nowadays the former did not necessarily have to be a condition before the latter. Not that he approved. When he was a young man it was seen as shameful to have a child out of wedlock.

He had bought a notebook which he entitled, 'Covid Culprits', underlining it with a red pen. On the first page he listed the government guidelines to the conduct of the population during the lockdown, with the title *Rules*. On the next page, he listed all the occupants of the road in chronological order, with their names printed at the side leaving plenty of room for any misdemeanours he should encounter, to be noted.

He found an old pair of binoculars in the loft which he dusted down. Never throw anything away, you never know when it might come in handy. He positioned himself on a straight backed dining chair that gave him a clear view of the road. To get to the town the occupants on the road would have to pass his house. Excellent.

He had brought up with him a travel kettle filled with water, tea bags, biscuits, milk and sugar. So, all prepared, Alfred waited.

It wasn't long before he saw Anne from no: 3 leave her house and walk past at a leisurely pace, talking into her phone as she strolled along. He made a note of the time, 10.30am. He checked the list of rules. An hours exercise once a day.

Shortly afterwards he witnessed Pauline from no. 20 appear from her garage, close it and wait in her front garden. Arthur leaned forward, who was this walking towards Pauline. He used his binoculars. It was Carolyn from no. 22. She was making straight for Pauline and… yes they were walking up the road together. He checked the rules again. You can only take your exercise with another member of the same household. They were blatantly breaking the rules. He quickly wrote this down in the Covid Culprits' notebook.

He had hardly finished this before he was using the binoculars again. There were three boys on large-wheeled bikes, tearing down the pavement doing wheelies not allowing any social distancing between themselves and the pedestrians. He didn't need to look at the rules to know it should be two metres. He recognised one of the boys. He was Mrs Oswald's eldest son from no. 32. Shouldn't she be home schooling him not allowing him to cycle off with his mates? He noted all this, emphasising the fact that they had broken more than one rule. *Bring back National Service,* he thought, *that would instil some discipline into them.*

Sighing, he turned the kettle on for his morning cup of tea. Waiting for it to boil, he kept his eye on the road. Down the middle of the pavement came a jogger, panting, sweating and grunting with the effort, Brian from no. 16 was obviously returning from an unaccustomed run. He made no effort to move out of the way from Clair no. 27 and then Sheila from no. 35 who were also on their way for some exercise oblivious to the danger of walking through Brian's potentially disease spreading breath. *If they would only put their phones down for a few minutes and concentrate on their safety, this would not be happening,* he thought. He wrote this all down.

Alfred realised that he had not yet seen anyone wearing a mask. He checked his information again. These had definitely been recommended by the government. He had made his out of a J cloth and a piece of elastic for the ear loops. He had better make a note of that.

A car drawing up next door prompted him to take out his binoculars again. He gasped. It was his neighbour's son, his wife and three children. He watched in horror as they all piled out, pulling shopping bags from the boot. His neighbours had opened up the front door and were coming down the path to greet them. Alfred nearly dropped his binoculars in shock. They were hugging each other. He got the notebook and scribbled it all down. He knew they lived in Colchester an hour away, another rule broken, you should not do long journeys. Thank goodness he would be able to tell them where they were going wrong. They obviously had not read the guidelines.

He glanced at his watch. 12.30pm, time for lunch soon. He was loath to leave his post though. Then he realised Anne had not yet returned. She had been out for two hours, an hour over the prescribed time. She would need reminding of this. He was going to have to use his Covid emergency weapon, a megaphone he had acquired online. It was only £11.99 and anyway who else had he to spend his money on? A bit less for the nephews and nieces and their children who he never saw from one year to the next, who would suddenly appear out of the woodwork once he had popped his clogs. He left his post to grab the instrument from a box in the corner then repositioned himself.

It wasn't until 1pm that Anne walked round the corner. Alfred threw open his window and using the megaphone he called out, "Anne you have taken two and a half hours to complete your walk. Did you not realise it is only supposed to be an hour?"

Anne literally jumped, letting out a cry of terror she looked round, clutched her chest and then much to Alfred's surprise, collapsed in an undignified heap on the pavement.

Alfred realised he was breaking every rule in his Covid Culprit's book. There was not two metres between him and Anne and he touched her without gloves, a mask or an apron as he searched for a pulse. He did not comment as passers-by crowded round him, using their phones to ring an ambulance to take her to the A&E department of the nearest hospital you were supposed to avoid having to use because of the risk of infection.

Flight Lieutenant Alfred Richards felt very depressed as he watched Anne, who at last had regained consciousness, disappear up the road in an ambulance with the lights flashing. What had started up being a well meant Neighbourhood Watch Scheme had turned into a disastrous Neighbourhood Botch Scheme.

A Deeper Shade of Blue

Dawn Knox

Blue eyes stared up in an unwavering gaze at the mother.

The baby girl had been born into a world gone mad. An England in lockdown and a house shut off from family and friends. Other than her parents, she's seen no one and her mother wondered if she remembered the midwives in gowns, masks and glasses being there at her beginning. If she did, would she assume they were a dream?

Did she dream?

Home was peaceful; punctuated only by her cries when she felt hunger or discomfort. But when she was contented, her mother took her into the garden and imitated the birdsong, tuning her ears to the sounds all around. There were more birds. Or perhaps they were louder.

She laid the baby on her back to kick her legs and look up.

Scientists said the sky appeared to be bluer now than it had before her birth – as blue as her eyes.

"Fewer fumes," they said.

"Less pollution," they said.

One day, her baby's eyes would change from blue to some other colour.

One day, when lockdown was lifted and normal life returned, the sky would fade to a paler shade of blue.

"More fumes."

"More pollution," they would say.

Unless, of course, normal life didn't resume.

Perhaps mankind might discover it preferred a deep, blue sky.

At the beginning of her child's life, the mother could only guess at what the future might bring. New vocabulary and phrases had been introduced: 'Coronavirus', 'COVID-19', 'Flattening the curve', 'R zero', 'Lockdown', 'When will it end?'

The mother had gifted her child a word for this time.

That word was her name.

She'd called the baby, Hope.

One More Story

Hannah Retallick

She hugs him. Real tight. The bunny who cared for her when she was born, brought by an auntie's nervous hand and placed beside the sleeping baby.

She tickles his ears. Floppy, damp with tears, stained with dust from the floor he was dragged across. Mummy had never killed him in the washer, drowned his stuffing in the sink, or passed a wipe across his face.

She whispers in his ear. He understands non-words – always did and always will. Black beady eyes, reflecting the naked bulb. He's crying, Mummy. I'm sorry, my love, I must.

She strokes his head. Don't cry, Floppy, please don't cry, you're making me cry. Jessica, come on now.

She loses her hold. No, Mummy, no. My love, you'll get him back when I'm done – I promise he'll be okay. Promise. Now, wash your hands, my love, wash your hands.

A Star Pupil of the Isolation Age

Hannah Retallick

April 9th 2020

I stand in the kitchen making a salad. Glancing out of the window, I see a man walk past. His walk speaks to me. It speaks loudly and clearly.

"Hello," it says. "I am a man who is walking down the road. I'm walking down the road in a ceremonial fashion because it has become deeply significant of late. There is something I must make clear: it's my first walk of the day. And you know what? It's my ONLY walk of the day. I hope my serious expression is enough to convince you of this. I am a highly responsible individual who would, under no circumstances, steal another helping of exercise, or otherwise flout government regulations.

You know what else I am? I am Staying Away from People. Like, so far away from people. No one is more socially distant than me. I am walking in the middle of the road, an empty road, frenetically scanning the estate landscape in case I suddenly come face to face with humans as they carelessly step out of their houses. I am the very model of* a man who's ready to leap left or right as the situation requires. Sorry to go 'Girl Guides' on you, but… BE PREPARED."

This man is well out of view by now. You might wonder how I can glean all this from swinging arms and tight shoulders and striding legs. Well, I can't really, but I can guess, can imagine – and isn't imagining the most fun thing ever? Imagining makes me smile as I toss freshly chopped tomatoes into my salad.

---

* …a Modern Major-General. (Shout out to Gilbert and Sullivan.)

Removing Social Masks

S. Nadja Zajdman

Of Thursday, April 23, 2020 in Montreal, Canada

I went to the little fruit and veggie place on Cote St. Luc Road. *Soleil*, it's called. It's run by a toothless old Turk, his son Ely, and a black helper named Albert. I discovered this place before winter. It's a hole in the wall in the middle of nowhere, but the produce has always been of superior quality, and the atmosphere was friendly.

When I arrived there was a line-up in front of the door. A short one. Because the place is so small, now only two customers are allowed in, at a time.

I came up Cote St. Luc Road wheeling my trolley. Because of the pain in my leg, I was walking more slowly than usual. Because I had to wheel the trolley, I didn't carry a cane.

A young, petite, dark-haired woman wearing a mouth mask got out of a solid-looking white car parked in front of the store, and scooted in front of me. "Looks like a tie," I said. She gave me a hard stare. She had pretty dark eyes. The mask covered the rest of her face. "Beauty before age." She ignored my hint, and planted herself in front of me, at a distance.

While waiting, this woman got on her cell phone. From the inflection and quality of both her French and English, it was clear to me that she was a Moroccan Jewess. The Masked Moroccan went into the store ahead of me, but my turn came soon, so we were in the store at the same time. Quietly I selected my items. I noticed that, since this lockdown, the quality of the produce has deteriorated. It was obvious that The Masked Moroccan was a regular customer. At the very least she was a valued customer and, it would turn out, also a valuable one.

Ely, the youngish son of the Toothless Turk, began a conversation with The Masked Moroccan. It may not have been a flirtation, but it was a dance. Ely began the conversation by saying, "My brother is now on the Covid ward."

I was startled.

To The Masked Moroccan he clarified. The grocer's brother is a doctor, working in a private hospital in Turkey. "He was offered a position here, but he can make a lot more money there, and the weather can't be beat."

Is that the reason why one becomes a doctor? It seemed Ely knew that The Masked Moroccan is a medical person. Supposedly she is a nurse who now is working from home. (How does a nurse work from home?) Her husband is a cancer surgeon at the Jewish General Hospital.

Listening to this conversation distracted me and slowed me down. The impression I got was that the grocer was trying to impress the wife of a surgeon that he, too, was related to a doctor. Talking slowed down The Masked Moroccan even more than it slowed me down and, it turned out, she had a lot more shopping to do than I did, because she was shopping not only for her immediate family, which includes children, but also for her mother and aunt.

While The Masked Moroccan took her time with shopping and conversation, the queue outside the door got longer. An angry voice was raised and pierced the closed doors. "What's going on in there? When are we going to get in!"

From behind the counter, at the cash, the Toothless Turk sprang into action. He turned on ME. "Hurry up!"

I headed to the cash, but once more The Masked Moroccan sprung in front of me. "We're all in the same boat," she announced, serenely.

Once more, I had to wait behind her. The Masked Moroccan's order was massive. My wait was long, but my order was processed quickly. When I wheeled my loaded trolley down the steps and came outside I saw that a very long queue had formed. Several people in the line were blacks. Poor blacks. The Masked Moroccan swanned onto the street, her arms empty, while the black helper Albert lugged what appeared to be a dozen bags to her solid white car.

"Discrimination!" a black man, or woman, screamed from the

middle of the queue. (Hard to tell, under the mouth masks.) "It's discrimination!"

Oblivious, The Masked Moroccan glided into her car and sailed away. It was the young grocer who had to deal with the fall-out, and he did. Ely leapt onto the steps that led to the little store and planted himself firmly in front of what was developing into an angry mob. "Discrimination?" he bellowed, as Black Albert hid in the shop. "You know me! Do I do discrimination?" (I don't know. Do you do windows?) "In my neighbourhood I had to wait two hours before getting into IGA! If you don't want to wait, you can go!"

The skinny, skin-headed grocer with fierce dark eyes quivered. He was genuinely unconscious of the part he played in creating this scene by favouring one wealthy, self-centred customer over a line of others. "Nobody gives me a hard time!"

There was grumbling among the masses. I decided to high-tail it down Cote St. Luc Road before a race riot broke out.

I wasn't in the same boat as The Masked Moroccan. I wasn't even in the same car. I had to wait for a bus to take me back to my side of the neighbourhood. When I got home I exchanged my trolley for a cane and went back outside to walk. Then I sat silently in the library garden. I remained in silence for the rest of the day. So this is it, I thought. This is the way it's going to be for the foreseeable future, and a foreseeable future is all I've got. I'll never travel overseas, again. I'll never see more of the world, before leaving it. All I'm going to get is trips to grocery stores, where I'll witness scenes such as this one.

Latte-less in the Time of COVID-19

Shelley Keats

April 27, 2020

I'm suffering from being SIP-ed. Since I was ordered to Shelter-in-Place and wear a mask, there have been no morning lattes at Zincs. Zincs is where I get my a.m. caffeine and gossip fix. Usually, I pick an empty seat at an already occupied table because most people don't have the gumption to refuse me. Then I pull out a copy of *The Times*, and doesn't have to be current. Sometimes, I just drag along last week's so I don't have to fork out another two quid along with the cost of the latte. I'm careful not to use a local rag. That way, people think I'm probably from out of town.

Absorbed behind my paper screen, I pretend to be reading. After a few minutes, I've become invisible, the proverbial fly on the wall. You can imagine the juicy tidbits that sail around me.

"Julie's been having an affair with that lawyer for almost a year now, and Dick still hasn't noticed. I wish I had one of those work-a-holic husbands."

"Did you see Frank in that Speedo on Sunday? I don't know where he gets the chutzpah with those rolls around his middle."

At times there's just one other someone at the table. I still dive into *The Times*. Usually they'll pick up their smartphone. Texting has become the bane of my café life. As you can imagine, reading what's being thumb thumped from behind *The Times* isn't a snatch. Putting down the paper to make conversation while straining to read what's been written became the new challenge until COVID-19.

So thwarted by the SIP decree am I, that, I've taken to stationing myself beside the neighbour's fence. The best time is after dark while sipping a brandy-laced coffee. Sammy's girlfriend, a petite goodie two shoes, meets him for a non-social distancing tryst. There's not much dialogue, but the soundtrack is pretty good.

This SIP thing has nearly stopped my gossip train in its tracks; I am desperately looking for a fix.

The Choice – April 2020

Mary Bevan

Two worlds sit side by side. Outside locked gates fear stalks unchallenged, streets emptied, suspicion loiters; somewhere in a distant menagerie a lion bellows. She feels the sensuous slide of cool silk on her skin, remembers the spit and toil and rumbling boil of the miracle grub in its white cocoon, the humping of the caterpillar, the dance of the butterfly, the days that are too long though they rush by. She prises the window open with a blunt knife, cracking old paint, graunching unoiled hinges, hears the music of the birds, sees the sunrise over a storm-dark sea, watches battling cloud dragons slowly disintegrate – into swans.

May

Reprieve

Doug Hawley

It started in January of 1990, but the exact date is unknown. George Bush was the US president. The Soviet Union was disintegrating and its satellite states were going their own way. African American politicians experienced mixed success – David Dinkins was elected mayor of New York City and Marion Barry was arrested in Washington DC. A bright light was the beginning of the Simpsons on Fox TV.

The world was experiencing its normal quota of evil and not exactly evil.

No one knew it then, but cyanic had left Africa months ago. What made cyanic different from other plagues was that it had an extremely long latency period during which it was communicable, but showed no symptoms. The public had no idea how far the disease had spread until most of the world had been infected. By the time the disease was understood, there was no treatment and most people were doomed.

The first symptom of cyanic was a slightly blue tinge to the skin, hence the scientific name. Most people referred to the victims as 'having the blues'. Within a week of the color change people started to act like the zombies from the George Romero films and lost cognitive function. Later research found that cyanic hit the higher brain functions first. Unlike movie zombies, cyanics had no taste for brains, or for any food. They just shambled pointlessly until they died.

Researchers determined that cyanic was spread by skin to skin contact. A grim humorist was quick to start the 'Six degrees of cyanics' game. No one affected was amused.

Pundits noted that it was a case of life imitating art. There were comparisons to Captain Trips in Stephen King's *The Stand* and the Wandering Disease in the old movie *Shape of Things* based on the works of H.G. Wells.

As usual, before the disease hit its stride, there were the usual conspiracy theories. Jews were blamed, because Jews are blamed for everything. It didn't hurt that the Israelis were less affected than other areas. Sunnis blamed the Shias, the Shias blamed the Sunnis. Before being decimated, there was even more Moslem on Moslem violence than usual. Survivalists saw black helicopters everywhere. Some Christians saw it as God's judgement on secular society and homosexuality in particular. A minority of the people believed the scientists' explanation that cyanic arose as a mutation of the Ebola virus. The explanation was particularly derided by those who did not believe in evolution at all.

The more serious also played the blame game. Environmentalists said in essence, "I told you so" as did the anti-immigration people. Those from the more rabid animal rights groups said it was fair because we had been exploiting non-human animals for far too long. A man who had predicted the demise of humans in the next hundred years admitted to being a little optimistic.

Some of those who were exposed had natural immunity. Some, particularly isolated farmers, did not come in contact with the affected. At the other end, large cosmopolitan cities were affected the worst. All of the major world capitals were depopulated. Second tier cities and the 'flyover' cities did much better. Portland Oregon, Salt Lake City, Kansas City, Des Moines, Knoxville and Pittsburgh fared relatively well.

As the enormity of the plague became clear, disposal teams were organized. Huge pits were dug and crews in hazmat suits herded walking cyanics into them.

The plague started to subside after a few months and eventually stopped. The cause of cyanics died or mutated again. By that time most of the world's population had died. By then the estimated world population had decreased from over five billion to well under a billion. Asia, Africa and South America were particularly hard hit, but no continent had over a quarter of its previous population.

Aside from the horror, life was horrible and wonderful. There were huge stores of food, petrol, cars, appliances and homes that inundated the remaining humans. As expected, liquor and appliance stores were looted. Because the world militaries and governments were disproportionately depleted, people could just take what they wanted. Eventually most people decided that there was little point in having five cars and three houses, and shared reasonably. This was after a few more million had died fighting over the spoils. As always a few thought that they deserved more, but there were no more African women walking ten miles to get water, the survivors just moved closer to the water, since there was no one there to chase them off. Various means in different communities were used to distribute desirable possessions of the departed. In some places lotteries were used. In other places, it was whoever got there first.

In most of the world, the remaining people gathered around city states and tribes. Such arbitrary borders in Belgium, the Middle East and much of Africa evolved over time. Ethnic minorities in Asia went their own way. China split into five different regions that didn't acknowledged the others' existence. English-speaking North America formed a very loose confederation. A minor surviving official in the US claimed that he was the ruler, but was totally ignored. The worldwide partitioning was much easier than the Pakistan – India split years earlier.

The loosely knit North America included Columbia consisting of the Northwest, Alaska, British Columbia and Northern California. It resembled Ecotopia in an old novel. A major product was cannabis. Mexicali consisted of Southern California, Nevada, Arizona, New Mexico and some of West Texas. The rest of Texas never got reorganized. Vast portions of the Canadian and US plains became Range. US upper Midwest states and Ontario became, after much debate Lake Land, although some chose to call it Heart Land. Louisiana, Utah, Florida, Quebec and Colorado retained much of their original boundaries. The South not a part of something else went back to Dixie. What was left of the US and Canada became New England.

The regions differed on abortion, minimum wage, anti-discrimination, but had no national authority to overturn their decrees. Utah at least tacitly accepted polygamy, but not same-sex marriage. Most of the former North America did the opposite.

These quasi-governmental areas evolved over a number of years and made a lot more sense than the original state and province boundaries.

Because of the fear of new plagues and a desire for self-sufficiency there was much less trade than before. The former Soviet Union and the Middle East suffered greatly when the demand for gasoline and natural gas dropped like a rock in sync with the population. A positive side effect was that there wasn't enough money to buy hordes of weapons. The major weapons exporters had quit manufacturing anyway. There was some minor scuffling over petty grievances and the need for arable land, but mostly people just moved to their own kind and found a way to feed themselves.

There were a few years when most people didn't worry about work or how to survive. Car breaks down? Get a new one. Need food? Go to the grocery store and take whatever canned food you want. Don't like your home? Move into a new one.

There were some occupations that were still necessary. Farmers had to grow food, trains and truckers were needed to move thing things, and people needed to operate utilities. With the much lower need for food, some farmers quit and moved to town, others continued as they had and some moved from marginal land to more fertile areas. In some cases people who got bored just picked up some of the required jobs. Jack Wiggins in London didn't see any need to be a corporate lawyer, so he started being a railroad engineer. He was lucky not to kill anyone, but eventually he got the hang of it.

At the end of the plague, the largest cities in the North America were Calgary, Indianapolis and Portland OR in that order. All had a little over a hundred thousand people. Calgary continued to be the energy center, Indianapolis evolved into the lead manufacturing site, and Portland moved from being a minor player in entertainment and electronics to the leader in the Americas. The previously major cities were ghost towns.

Zero population adherents were pleased by the lower number of humans, if not how it had happened. Some traditional male Catholics, Muslims and Mormons saw the situation as an opportunity to dominate the world by rapid reproduction. The women were not as enthused.

Energy production and pollution were greatly reduced by much smaller use of the energy sources. For a while a lot of people wanted to get the biggest Suburbans, Land Cruisers, Rolls, Bentleys and Mercedes they could find, but that got old after a while. The energy needs of earth were scaled down roughly in proportion to the population drop. An added advantage was that there were plenty of sources for energy without using the more polluting forms such as coal.

Because entertainers and producers didn't have much need for money and the stars were mostly deceased, local talent and local *no talent* took over television, radio and the stage. The results were mixed. There were Paul Newmans and Meryl Streeps who simply hadn't been discovered, as well Joe Plum, who had a post-plague short-lived TV show in which he talked about his coin collection. There were all porn channels, golf channels, romance channels, run by amateurs or low level professionals. Into this mix, Janet Levitz from the Bay Area and Thane Gibbons, a Portland native, wandered into the mix. Their bright idea, concocted and run in Portland, was InVid, a video sharing service.

David Nelson Hilliard was intrigued by InVid. He saw it as his way to become a star. After he recalled that he had no talent, he revised his thinking to believe that he would become a world leader. To say that he had a Napoleonic complex would be an insult to Napoleon. His lack of looks was compensated for by his lack of height. He was, however, a forward thinker and saw a way to profit from the new world order and even attract some girls. After a few hours of intense work he had a plan to rule the world.

The next day he had his tall dark and handsome neighbor Doug record the Hilliard Manifesto on InVid as well as calling as many world state leaders as possible.

"New Earth arises from Old Earth tested and improved. From

this, the worst tragedy in human history, we gain our reprieve from impending disaster. For if the plague had not wiped out much of the earth's human population, we would have soon done the job ourselves. Deforestation, ocean acidification, global storming, overpopulation, mass human caused extinctions and pollution were the stepping stones to human extinction."

"Now we have to ask, will we repeat the same mistakes? I say no and I have a program to give us a few million more years of dominion on planet earth. The United Nations died with the pre-plague earth. Let us start a new organization consistent with the new reality. I propose World Harmony."

"The states in World Harmony will agree to:

> Assist neighbors in need if able;
>
> Refrain from acts of aggression against my neighbors or supporting a national army;
>
> Allow immigration if economically practical;
>
> Allow emigration;
>
> Support World Harmony Armed Forces;
>
> Assist in the defense of states under attack; and
>
> Obey the decisions of the World Court.

After joining World Harmony, states may be expelled by the World Court."

"National leaders may wonder what advantage you might gain from membership in World Harmony. You will get protection from aggressive neighbors and assistance in an emergency. The price that you pay is fairly small."

For months there was no response. Then there was a trickle of positive responses. After a couple of years most of the post-plague nations had signed up. Some of them remembered the United Nations as a positive, if not perfect institution and wanted a replacement. Others liked the simple set of rules. A number of states didn't like their existing borders, and decided to stay out.

As the instigator, Hilliard set himself up as the first Governor of World Harmony in 1995. The headquarters was in an abandoned bank in downtown Portland. The World Court was organized the following year. The member states formed World Harmony military bases on each continent.

In 1997 World Harmony was tested for the first time. The minor states of the former Burma – Kachin, Karen, Muslim Region and others – were attacked by the majority Burmese state, Myanmar. World Harmony forces from Mumbai were able to restore order and expel Myanmar from World Harmony; with the promise that Myanmar could reapply for admission after proving that it had disbanded its illegal army. Thereafter, World Harmony was taken seriously.

Post-plague earth went along fat and happy for a few years using up the assets left over from before the plague. Governor Hilliard, in particular was fat and happy. His status had indeed gotten him girls or women – those with low esteem and those that wanted to get close to power. His favorite was Rose Reed, who knew how to flatter and please him. Just as some say you can't cheat an honest man, manipulators are often manipulated. In June of 1999 Jacque Braque of New France called Hilliard and suggested they were living on borrowed time. It was fortunate that Braque spoke better English than Hilliard did.

"Governor Hilliard, you have done a great job so far, keeping the world peace. However, we have serious challenges ahead of us. At some point the old cars, appliances will break down, utilities will need maintenance and housing will fall apart. Something else that you may not be aware of, many computers will fail in January because they will not recognize the year 2000. Not only do we have a challenge, we have an opportunity, we can improve on our lives compared to before the plague. We have the chance for a do over."

Now Hilliard wasn't smart and he didn't understand the implications of what Braque had said. Hilliard thought everything was fine because he had the love (or so he thought) of several resourceful and beautiful women, all he could eat and drink and the admiration of millions. He was, however, manipulative and lazy.

"Mr. Braque, you and I are entirely in sync. I was just saying to an assistant today, we need to plan for the future. The name that came up repeatedly to head up the effort was yours. Consider that you have a blank check written by me to plan for the future."

"Thank you Governor. I already have tentative plans."

Hilliard immediately put out the word that his assistant would be implementing Hilliard's plan to improve the world's future.

Braque knew that Hilliard would want all the credit, but was willing to proceed anyway.

In Braque's mind, engineering was the easy part, politics was the hard part. Towards that end, he asked for planners and engineers from all of the world's states. After interviewing them, he knew which to use and which to work around. Whichever category they fell in, the contributions of all of them and their states would be highly praised.

After a get-to-know-you party for all of them, he outlined his plans.

"As you all know we are currently living on credit. We can have a bright future or fall into darkness. It is up to us. My plan:

> Those who live in dangerous places subject to flooding, hurricanes, drought or monsoons should move to safer available places.
>
> Fishing and forestry must be sustainable. In fact, our forests and fish stocks must be replenished.
>
> We should move to renewable energy sources such as tidal, solar and wind. I depend on all of you here to do the research and building as necessary.
>
> Vehicles should be made to be practical and run by either electricity or something better if we can come up with it. As much as possible, they should be recyclable.
>
> Each region should be self-sufficient. If this is impractical in some cases, we should provide assistance as necessary.
>
> We must avoid overpopulation, which was part of the cause of the plague.
>
> Rivers should run free and with the depopulation, there should be huge animal reserves. Threatened African wildlife and buffalos in the US can make a comeback.

I know that there will be resistance to these ideas in some quarters. 'What about my house at the shore? Will I still have a cell phone?' There may be some sacrifices, but I think that we can sell a better future, and yes you can still have a cell phone. If you have a house at the coast, no one will insure it. So before we start, you have to sell the plan to your people, if indeed you are on board.

Questions or comments?"

"Yes Ms. Sebastian of Chile?"

"Your plan sounds good, but what benefits will my country get?"

"Correct me if I'm wrong, but I believe that your country imported crude oil before the plague and now you are having difficulty obtaining supplies. We want you to be able to produce your own energy and fuels indigenously."

"Mr. Kralic of Bosnia?"

"Will your government people interfere with our customs or government?"

"Depends on what you mean. In general, no. If your state should produce an unsustainable population, or over exploit your resources, you will not be in the program and you will not be receiving our assistance. Is that clear?"

"All too clear."

"Now if you would, we have arranged for all of you to join tables with facilitators to answer your questions and take your comments."

Several hours and bathroom, snack and drink breaks, the state leaders left with a fairly clear idea of what Mr. Braque's plan was. Most were in favor, but there were a few dissenters. The somewhat diminished China was not sure about blowing up its major dams. The North America Columbia region was ambivalent about losing the dams that provided most of the region's electricity.

Mr. Braque had his engineers draw up scenarios for the dissenters showing how they would come out ahead by moving their constituents to safer areas, letting rivers and forests return to their state before the industrial revolution, and replacing coals burning power plants by solar, wind and tidal power. They also showed how much the energy needs would be decreased by some simple changes, for example replacing much of the heating and cooling of houses by circulating water underground and then back through the houses. Most of the world states bought it. Some that distrusted anything smacking of Western culture were hold outs.

With most of the world on board, Braque made a five-year-timeline for what he was convinced was a way to keep the planet going for a long time. The next few years would see a modest beginning to a lessening of the extinction of flora and fauna and pollution.

The first step, replacing computer legacy programs before the year 2000 was easier than expected.

Rose was immediately attracted to Jacque's intelligence and looks, particularly compared to Hilliard. The only thing that Jacque was missing was Hilliard's power. She made sure that they bumped into each other, literally in some cases, from time to time. Jacque, whose wife had died in the plague, was interested.

The morning after meeting in a local motel, they discussed the future. They had been too busy to talk the night before.

"Tell me, Rose, how that buffoon could become the most powerful man in the world. His World Harmony idea looks like it was taken from a cereal box, or an episode of *GI Joe*."

"I think that it was a Cheerios box. He had three things going for him. He got the timing right. He had a feel for attracting the right people. He is a master manipulator. Oh yeah, four things – he was incredibly lucky."

"Are you satisfied being his number one consort?"

"Hell no, it was just the best deal I could make at the time. I admit it; I was looking for my main chance. You tell me something. Are you happy letting somebody you call a buffoon treat you as his lowly assistant?"

"As you say, hell no."

"I know with certainty that Hilliard will die in the next few months, are you ready to plan for his exit?"

"How do you know that, Rose?"

"You're better off if you don't know. Here is my question for you, Jacque, are you ready to take over World Harmony with me? I've already arranged to be married to him before he dies, that will give us some legitimacy from the get go."

"I can't think of a better team than you and I. How do you know he will marry you?"

"He's so insecure. I just told him I'd leave if he didn't. When he is gone, after a reasonable mourning period, we get married. Our ascension will be almost a coronation. I've already lined up support within the government. I've been running several departments for months. Can you get your engineering staff behind you?"

"Easy."

Fifty days after this conversation Hilliard was dead. As Reed had indicated, taking over was easy. Hilliard had been seen as a figurehead for at least a year, and people were used to working with Reed and Braque. Their marriage a month after Hilliard's death sealed the deal.

A decade later there were clear improvements in land, sea and air. Many formerly endangered species were thriving. There were few conflicts between modern conveniences and the ecology. The world population had only increased only 2% since the plague. There were a few local conflicts, but nothing major. Reed and Braque had a son and a daughter, who were in training to run the world when the time was right. In a self-congratulatory mood, Rose said to Jacque, "I was thinking we should declare a Thousand Year Reich, but that might not sound right."

"Right, but we should get our PR people to work on that, see what they can come up with."

"It is hard for to believe how this has turned out for me. I was always smarter than the other guys, but people only paid attention to my body. That's where Hilliard screwed up. If he had given me more credit, he might still be around."

"I had it tough too. I was always scorned as the French version of a nerd. Nobody wanted to hear me talk about anything except other scientists. If she'd lived longer, my wife would have left me."

"And here we are at the head of a dynasty."

The phone rang.

After listening for a while, Reed blanched. When she hung up she said, “This is very bad.”

“I couldn’t be worse that what we’ve been through the last ten years.”

“It could and it is. An asteroid is heading towards earth.”

All Together Now

Linda Morse

This set of five radio monologues was written during the Covid-19 pandemic 'Lockdown' 2020.

PART 1 THE DEVIL'S INSTRUMENT

(Nicole is having a complete melt-down. She is attempting to take deep breaths and control herself. There is the continuous tuneless tooting of a recorder)

Hi Julie, I'm having a melt-down. Can't get you on WhatsApp. Please ring.

(To herself) Please, pleeeease ring…

I love my kids.

I love my kids.

But that bloody recorder is driving me insane. What's that crash?

"What are you doing? I'm on the phone." Nearly.

"Max! Stop blowing that…" He's gone.

I LOVE MY KIDS!

"Finley's trying to work!"

Isn't he? It's his GCSE year next year.

Oh my God they sound as though they're killing each other. The phone!

Julie, thank goodness. Are you coping? I'm losing it… I'm truly losing it…

…

But I'm a useless Mum. Really, really I am.

I know what I'm supposed to be doing.

Establishing a daily routine, because it's good for children. Makes them feel secure.

OKAY! I KNOW ALL THAT. I AM TRYING!

Sorry I'm shouting aren't I?

I'm getting stressed…

I just need to talk.

And possibly eat chocolate.

Oh thank you… thank you. You are just the person I need.

You see, I spent yesterday evening after everyone was in bed (except Finley who was still on his Xbox, playing a virtual game with some 'mates' he actually doesn't know.) Honestly. Really. I spent the whole evening planning a good 'lockdown' routine:

One – Start the day with a proper, unrushed, nourishing breakfast.

Two – Exercise all together as a family.

Three – All settle down to do our work.

Working from home is so hard, isn't it? And Finley and Jessica both have a ridiculous amount sent home from school. Max… well Max is only five, after all. I think he might be a problem. Max is Max and… well you know…

Anyway… the plan was work would take us to… lunchtime.

Number four on my list – Wholesome, homemade soup, followed by:

Five – A quiet time – reading, writing stories, day-dreaming, NO TV.

Six – Family activity time, a game or something creative all together.

Then Seven – Everyone plays and entertains themselves until dinner.

Oh Julie, it sounded so good at midnight last night, but even by eight o'clock this morning, I could see it would all fall apart.

Breakfast went well, apart from a spat about whether everyone HAD to have porridge. I promised muesli and blueberries tomorrow, I forgot I'm pretty much out of fresh fruit.

We started with the family exercises in the garden. It was a bit chilly, but the sun was out. I thought we could have a go at yoga.

Have you tried yoga?

Oh… I thought you might have some tips.

Apart from the exercise, I've heard that it's very calming and children really relate to it.

I found what looked like a really fun YouTube video, all joggling, coloured letters and bouncy music and this slim, American blonde, you know the type all legs and amazing make-up…

I haven't worn make-up for ages. Have you?

…

It doesn't seem worth it, does it?

So this yoga teacher:

(Yoga Teacher American accent) Hi I'm Selina – Jayne. Welcome to our fun Yoga class for kids. I'm so excited that you're here with us today. Why not let Mum and Dad join in too?

(Normal voice) Steve's at work. Lucky sod.

(Yoga teacher) "And here to help me are Maddi-Lyn and Tyler."

There were these two strange-looking children sitting in perfect cross-legged poses, smiling benignly and looking much cleaner than my kids.

Max was already covered in grass stains and twigs and he's painted his feet blue again. Why?

(Yoga teacher) "Say Hi Guys! Hi…iii. We're gonna start with Balloon Breathing."

At which point Jessica, got all excited. "Did you buy balloons, Mum, when you were panic buying in Tescos?"

I paused the video and snapped at her, "I wasn't panic buying!" But I was, wasn't I? We all were. I said, "No I didn't buy balloons. I was buying important things like… toilet rolls."

Then Finley chimes in, "And a lot of tinned tomatoes."

(Nicole) "You like tinned tomatoes"

Then Jessica becomes all ecstatic about how much she loves pasta.

(Aside) I couldn't get pasta.

Really? Oh I'll try them next time I'm allowed out.

No, I didn't handle it very well. I just screamed, not at all calmly, "We're doing a yoga class!" By this time American Beauty was on to

(Yoga teacher) "Breathe in with your nose and breathe out with your mouth… That's very good."

Now fill up your belly with air and—" At this point Max, said, "What's a belly?"

I did handle this bit well I thought. I paused the video… all full of Mummy goodness and replied with infinite patience.

"It's just another name for your tummy, darling." I was going to use it as an opportunity to talk about breathing deeply and using your diaphragm, but then Jess interrupted in that superior nine-year-old voice she does and just called him, "Stupid!" which rather shut down the conversation. I'm not sure she's as kind as I'd like her to be.

We struggled on with the yoga.

(Yoga teacher) "Now make sure you've got those legs all nicely crisscrossed. Well done. Now we're going to paint a rainbow."

We were *all* a bit confused by that.

"Stretch out your arm to one side and touch the floor and then, sweep it right over your head and down to the other side. There that's lovely and you've painted a rainbow."

Really? I mean do *you* think that's painting a rainbow?

(Nicole laughs) Yeah, I thought she was a complete loony by this time, but I couldn't say that, could I?

(Yoga teacher) "What colour is YOUR rainbow?"

Finley had that look of utter disdain that only a teenager can have. "This stuff is for little kids."

Jessica, of course, primly recited, "Red, Orange, Yellow, Green, Blue, Indigo and Violet."

And Max suggested, "Cow-poo colour"

Then he went off and found the recorder… under the gooseberry bush. A baby would have been so much quieter.

I honestly believe it was the devil who invented the recorder.

"Are we doing this yoga or not?" I snapped.

And the kids all said, "No."

PART 2 THE BOTTOM LINE

(Nicole is calm)

Hi Julie.

Thanks. Oh and Steve sends his love.

I think we've turned a corner with the kids. There were no major issues over the lack of blueberries for breakfast. In fact Jessica, bless her heart, said she preferred bananas anyway.

It's cold, isn't it? We ditched yoga for some straight-forward indoor exercises and we 'got it done' in five minutes. Then magically everyone disappeared to do their homework. Amazing isn't it?

Yes and me. It's quite pleasant sitting here looking out at the garden, nibbling chocolate. Smug's all curled up, purring loudly and dozing in the only patch of sunshine on the carpet.

So I'm settling down to work. You too?

How are you getting on with the boss's awful digital dictation?

I know. It's the same for me. Somehow I have to produce an intelligible letter to go out with this contract. Honestly solicitors are the worst people on earth at dictation, aren't they? Nothing they say comes out in simple English.

(To herself) It's very quiet. Before I start, should I check the kids, d'you think?

No you're right. Seize the moment.

Have a good day. Speak to you later. Byeee.

(To herself) It is VERY quiet. Maybe there's something wrong. Oh, for Heaven's sake, Nicole, pull yourself together, stop fussing!

It's no good. I can't concentrate. They're never this quiet. Max had a bit of a poorly tummy this morning. I'll just pop in to check.

(Nicole's voice off) "Switch it off! Now!" And, of course I get a chorus of "Oowh." I'm trying to be assertive, but fair and caring.

"Get your homework out. I'll come and help in a minute. How's your tummy, Max? Go and try to have a poo. Where's Finley?"

(Nicole shouts upstairs) Finley! Finley!

"He's playing on his X Box."

Jessica's the family snitch. I'm not sure it's a very nice trait, but it's quite useful at times.

(Shouts upstairs) Finley! Finley!

(To Jessica) Go and get your homework out, Jessica. No, not in here. In the dining room. I'm trying to work! This is our working time. Look, I put it on the *Family Timetable*. Number Three – We work until eleven o' clock and THEN we have a drinks break.

You can take a glass of water with you.

"I don't like water."

Water's good for you. Just GO!

(Shouts upstairs) Finley! Finley! You've got Maths to do.

There's a massive crashing as Finley bounds down the stairs. He arrives, wearing his Maths face.

"I can't do it, Mum. I'll never pass Maths. It's too difficult."

I do try to be sympathetic. I realise, only too well, how hard it is working at home.

"OK, love. Do some other homework then. I'll try to help you with the Maths later."

His sarcastic laugh is quite unnecessary, I feel.

"Finley, that's rude! I was quite good at—" But he interrupts with a caustic, "Did you get an A?"

"No I got a D… OK… We'll see if we can set Granny up on Skype."

(To herself) Ohhhh – that could be another nightmare…

Did you shut your bedroom door? If Max gets out through your window onto the roof—

Finley bounds off.

"Sorry, Mum. Forgot"

We've had the builders in, but of course they haven't finished and now they've disappeared altogether. So it's possible for the children to get out of Finley's window onto the flat roof.

Right… Try again. Oh my God the Zoom Meeting's starting.

(Speaking to work colleagues via Zoom.)

Good Morning. Hi. We're all well. Good.

Hi Sally, I love your curtains. Isn't it strange seeing inside everyone's homes?

Morning. Oh sorry. I'll get it back to you today. I had a small problem with downloading the contract. Oh and in your dictation.

And then, with perfect timing Max appears tooting the recorder loudly. Followed by the very clear announcement, "I've done a funny poo. It was really hot. Do you want to see?"

The entire meeting laughs and I try, in an insufficiently quiet undertone, to say, "Go away Max. I'm working!"

Jessica appears. She attempts to haul him out of the room – to the amusement of the whole office.

"No, Jess. Be careful. Don't just hoick him!"

(To herself) I try to look nonchalant. I'm a working MOTHER. We live in a tolerant, gender-equal society remember.

Julie is giving me an amused wink. She understands.

However, the boss is only mildly amused. We're continuing to discuss the contract. Accompanied by strange scratching sounds. I'm trying to ignore them, but the entire meeting is becoming aware. I wonder whether to turn off the sound. But then they won't hear me when I'm speaking. Smug is making an absolute meal of using her litter tray, *(sigh)* I intended to move into the other room. Scratch, scratch, scratch followed by intermittent avalanches of cat litter, flying into view. It feels as though it'll go on forever. Now she's sitting on the window ledge in full view of the screen, washing her nether regions. Massively embarrassed I mutter, "She's an 'indoor' cat. The road here's too dangerous for her to go out."

Pheeew. This is hard.

OK. Be patient. The online filing system… I'm trying to explain it to Toby, who's rather dense for a solicitor. This feels interminable. I wonder how Max's tummy is? And what's Smug doing behind my back. I can't keep turning or flicking the camera round to see. Molly, the boss's secretary, looks as disapproving as a prune.

Surely we must be nearly finished. Please make this stop before…

And the tooting recorder approaches…

Max marches in, doing a sort of goose-step, and announces dramatically to camera, "Mummy, I'm going upstairs to see if I can do a cold poo."

PART 3 DEVIOUS DEVICES

(SFX: Background shouting and recorder tooting throughout)

Will you be alright with that? Both working from home. Mind you, Julie, sometimes I think I could do with Steve being here to help with the kids.

Yes that must be nice, coffee and lunch together and some non-work communication.

(Ironically) As you can probably hear, at this end, everyone is settling down quietly.

The work-out didn't really work out this morning, so we abandoned it. Now we are supposed to be back to studying. We're all going to 'Get it done!' Where did we first hear that expression? It keeps coming back to haunt me like the echo of a long-lost time. Remember 'Get Brexit Done?' Does anyone even remember Brexit?

(Laughs) The good old days, where we had time to complain about politics and wonder how leaving the EU was going to affect our summer holiday.

Jessica has been directed to an educational website, so has Max, so has Finley, so has every one of several million school children and they're all crashing. Not the children. Actually they're all crashing too, but in a noisier sort of way.

You know I don't have horrendous hang-ups about technology. But the failure of technical devices to function on request and the way they abdicate all their responsibilities half-way through a meeting irritates me beyond belief.

...

It was Jessica's online learning I was dealing with this morning. She set everything up yesterday ready for today, so I didn't anticipate the first hurdle being a bleak 'name or password incorrect'. Well you know how bright Jessica is, very well organised and just doesn't get things wrong. If it'd been Max, whose passwords are things like 'Jelly Poo Batman 99999999999' – until I tell him to stop pressing 9s.

"I like nines. Can I press sixes then?"

But Jessica, I believe Jessica when she says, "I know my password is right" and then proceeds to show it to me, carefully written down in her sparkly colour-changing *Unicorn Diary*, in between her neatly written recipe for homemade slime and a detailed attempt at drawing a hedgehog.

Yes that's it, the one I put on Facebook. My sister unkindly suggested it looked more like a tortoise.

Eventually it works. The screen announces triumphantly 'You're signed in'. That took ten minutes!

We press 'Go to Key Stage Two'. And the blooming thing digests this request so slowly you'd think it's never received such a demanding question in its tiny robotic existence.

It finally moves on to the next page and we receive a trite little message saying, 'Daily lessons coming soon', giving a date at the end of NEXT MONTH. I was hoping this whole business would be over by the end of next month! The website promptly crashes and that's the end of online education for today. *(Big sigh.)*

Jessica has now disappeared happily to watch TV and… well what more can I do? I have to sort out Granny and Finley's Maths lesson next.

Have you ever felt more disconnected and been *so* connected?

Exactly. The day is a never-ending stream of WhatsApp, Skype, Zoom, Facetime, Snapchat, Twitter, Facebook, Messenger. We did a Family Zoom with my sister Jane and her husband and kids. They were all sitting there with amazing backdrops of palm trees and golden beaches. I haven't worked out how to make that happen. I felt quite inadequate… again.

I tried WhatsApping Granny, but she didn't answer and just rang me back later on the landline, saying how exhausting her day was, talking to all her friends. Anyway better go.

I sent her an invitation to Zoom and the instruction to just 'click on the link,' so with luck she should be about to give Finley his Maths lesson.

Speak to you later. Byeee.

And here she is! I'm quite proud of her.

"Well done, Mum. Brilliant."

Somehow I feel her. "Oh I love Zoom. I've been doing it for the last couple of months" is a bit of a put-down.

I only heard of it last week.

Finley hasn't arrived.

(Shouts upstairs) "Finley! Finley!"

"Finley! It's your Maths lesson!"

Nothing.

"Finley, Granny's on Zoom." That's enough to bring him bounding down the stairs with the enthusiasm of a young colt.

Shut your door!

Silence and then he bounds up again, slams the door with enough force to demolish the unfinished building works and leaps goat-like down the stairs. He's arrived, full of the sort of boy bounce and enthusiasm I rarely see since he's been 'doing teenage.'

Hi Granny. How are you?"

He loves my Mum. They get on so well and he's completely charming to her all the time. Sometimes it feels a bit unfair. I'm the one who clears up the dirty pants and sweaty T-shirts and who attempts to find matching socks. Somewhere there's a Sock City, a sort of footwear Legoland.

Anyway here they are chatting away. I realise, I can't see anything resembling paper, pen, calculator, or Maths homework. My mum has reached the same conclusion.

Smiling indulgently she enquires, "Are you all ready to start then, love?"

Finley looks somewhat shocked by the question.

"What?"

"Your Maths homework. Mum sent it to me, so I'm ready."

"Oh Yeah… No…"

Then he starts doing this sort of head swaying thing. Which is part of his Maths persona. It's really weird.

I've failed… again. In my concern to help 'poor, old Granny' to get to grips with technology, I have entirely forgotten to organise my bright and cheerful young son, who is now ambling around slowly and painfully, as if he is completely lost in his own house, vaguely wondering where he might find a pen.

At this point my mum says, "Sorry, Fin, I've got a video conference lined up in a few minutes. You get yourself organised love, and ring me back after lunch."

And off she goes.

A video conference?

PART 4 SCAVENGER HUNT

Sorry I didn't ring last night, Julie. I felt really guilty that I'd moaned at you yet again.

I know, but here I am complaining about my kids and you must miss yours so much. Skype just isn't the same is it?

When mine are grown up, I'll miss them too. What on earth will I do with time to hear myself think?

Anyway I'm determined to be positive today. We're ditching the timetable. To be honest, I was a bit shaken yesterday when Finley came away from his Maths session with Granny, looking quite upset and said he was so worried she might get sick, because she's old. Then Jessica, burst into tears and wailed, "She might die and then we wouldn't have a granny." Max started breaking the arms and legs off his robot… or was that later? Anyway I realised they're just as stressed as me. They're missing their friends. It's awful isn't it? But, then the most wonderful thing happened on Facebook. There was this gorgeous, kind, helpful, altogether brilliant headmaster…

No not gorgeous in that way… there wasn't a picture of him… just his message. He said, "It's absolutely not possible to manage home learning with primary-aged children and work from home at the same time." That was it. Isn't that amazing! He said, "Stop trying to be a Superhero." I feel like a cloud has lifted. I've never loved anyone so much in my whole life. Well except you, when you ring up and listen to me wailing. Oh and Steve, of course.

…

So today we're going to have some fun. I guess, I'll just have to work till late this evening.

I've planned a day of exploration. We're starting with a scavenger hunt. Max thinks it's great and said could he go and dress up. That inspired Jessica to disappear into her bedroom to find a costume. She loves Dora the Explorer. Finley looked at me, raised an eyebrow (that's a new thing) and said he'd rather do his Physics homework. It felt a bit like a punch in the stomach to my *Family Fun* idea, but I could hardly argue, could I?

(Laughs) Yes, listen to how quiet it is?

I'm all fired up, clasping my three copies of 'Mum's Adventure Scavenger Hunt' and all the children have gone to their rooms and I've time for a chat with you. I think I'm getting the idea.

Max is back… dressed as a pirate, complete with a parrot on his shoulder.

"I'm going to dig for treasure."

Good old Max.

I bought him the costume for Book Week.

He's gone. Off racing round the garden shouting, "Yo, ho, ho" and "Ah me hearties." Do modern pirates still say that sort of thing?

Here comes Jessica. She has some odd contraption on her head made of coat hangers and scarves and held together by hairbands. She said it's to protect her from mosquitos.

"Brilliant, darling. Off you go then. Out in the garden. Won't be a moment. I'm just saying goodbye to Julie."

(To Julie) I'll ring you tonight and tell you how we got on.

Byeee.

Before we start, a quick shout upstairs. "Finley! That doesn't sound like Physics."

To which I get the usual smart response, "I didn't say I was doing Physics. I said, I'd rather do Physics than a 'Scavenger Hunt'."

(Nicole sighs.) Stay positive. "Shut your door."

I head into the garden, which is green, blossoming and in fact more the temperature of mid-summer. I'm going to enjoy today. We all are.

"Here we are. You've each got a copy of Mum's Adventure Scavenger Hunt."

"Wow!" says Max. I can see they're impressed. Even Jessica admits, "It's quite good."

"The first few treasures are really simple. Find three different coloured stones."

Immediately Jess asks, "Why are they treasures?"

"Because you're going to find three fantabulous stones!"

"Yeah!" Sometimes a five-year-old's enthusiasm can be really gratifying. He races off round the garden.

Find a beautiful EMPTY snail shell.

Find a stick that looks like 'Stickman'

So far so good. At this point I get more creative.

Make a picture out of coloured leaves.

I thought I could see an opportunity to creep off for my chocolate fix, but Max pipes up, "You've got to do it too, Mummy."

It's quite meditative, peacefully building up my leaf design. This is what family life is meant to be like. In the sun, calmly creating, alongside my wonderful children.

There's an ear-piercing scream.

Jessica's hysterical. Max is jumping up and down, alternating tooting his recorder wildly with shouting, "Police! Police! Nee Naw Nee Naw"

I've no idea what's happening.

There's the answer… a massive rat running across the garden, terrified by all the noise. Running towards the house.

"Back door. Back door!"

Neither of the children translates that to mean, "The back door is open. Shut it or the rat might get into the house."

Max is tooting frenetically. "Nee Naw Nee Naw. Police!" and Jessica is completely hysterical.

"Stop screaming. It's not going to hurt you"

That's not entirely true in all circumstances, of course, but there's no time to explain that rats are scavengers and eat rubbish and carry diseases. I'll get round to that when I've discovered whether or not it's in the house. That's the direction Jessica is now running towards for safety.

Another scream.

OK, so it's in the house.

"Police! Police! Nee Naw Nee Naw." Toot, toot, toot.

Max is now inhabiting a world of gangsters and crime prevention.

Jessica is hiding in the shed and I am entering the house with trepidation.

(Shouts upstairs) "Finley! Finley!"

Nothing.

If Steve's not here, I tend to shout for Finley. He can be quite good in these situations.

(Shouts upstairs) "Finley! Finley!"

Smug looks at me with mild interest. And then back at the unusual visitor. The rat looks just like the people panic buying in Tesco's, as it rushes, to and fro in a state of frenzy.

I shout at Smug, "Well do something. You feline idiot!"

She looks mortified. I never shout at her. I shout at the children, but never the cat. She shoots out of the door.

"Nooo Nooo. You're an indoor cat!"

"Smug! Smug!"

She's disappeared into the bushes.

Do I look for the cat or get the rat out of my house?

"Police! Police! Nee Naw Nee Naw!" Toot, toot, toot.

Jessica's crying *and* screaming now, quite a loud combination, "Mummy… Mummy Smug's running away."

Deep breaths. Grab a long stick. Rattus is crouching terrified in the opposite corner. We eye each other up as we both consider our options. It makes a dash.

There's a crash.

It's trying to jump out through the closed window and knocked off Jessica's 'I love you Mummy' vase of flowers. And…

It's back in the corner.

Breathe… I'm walking slowly around the perimeter of the room, stick well in front of me and prod the miserable rodent in the direction of the back door.

It's out! The rat heads for the same bush as Smug. We all freeze. Will this be her finest hour?

There's a tense pause.

Then Smug strolls out. Blinks. And walks back into the house.

We all trail in behind her.

She finds a cushion that doesn't smell of rat, and curls up to go back to sleep.

Rampaging elephants crash from upstairs. Finley, currently man-of-the-house arrives to tackles the crisis.

"Yeah, what is it?"

(Nicole sighs.)

PART 5 IN CASE OF EMERGENCY

Hi Julie, A quick message to say, everyone loved your idea of creating a portrait gallery. We're all painting, even Finley. He's very good at Art. We're each doing a picture of someone else in the family. Jessica's painting me. She's not flamboyantly creative like Finley or Max. But she likes details and tries very hard to be accurate. She wanted to be slightly superior, of course, so she's doing a full portrait. Max and Finley are doing heads.

Anyway, they are all doing it. So thanks for that. Better go. See you at the staff meeting.

Finley and Max definitely didn't get their talent from me. "Mummy, you've made me look like a cabbage"

Thanks Max. Maybe being inventive with green was a bad idea.

Oh! Time to log in to Zoom.

"I've got a meeting now, kids. Just pin your pictures up on the board behind me, when they're finished. Everyone from the office will be able to admire them then." (And I won't look like such a rubbish mum. Finley's portrait of Jessica is amazing.)

'Morning.' Rain's a surprise, isn't it? Hi. Morning.

The staff meeting's progressing normally, nice and brisk. Thank goodness, because I'm beginning to hear 'off stage' rowing between Finley and Jessica already.

She stomps in behind me to pin up her picture and somehow the mood of the staff meeting changes. There's some furtive smirking from a couple of the young blokes and then outright laughter. I turn round. Oh Jessica! That is way too much detail! I rip the portrait off the display board, to even greater mirth from the virtual office. The boss feels that it's time to close the meeting and so do I.

Do I have a moment to breath? No, there's an approaching sound of tooting.

"What are we going next, Mummy? Can we play Hide and Seek?"

"Only inside the house, Max. It's pouring with rain."

I think Jessica's avoiding me. She and Max have disappeared to another room and Finley is drifting into what I think of as his 'arty state'. He's plugged into his music, dreamily painting beautiful shapes and colours and looking happy. It's lovely.

Meanwhile I'm still sweaty, embarrassed and angry. My boobs are definitely not *that* big!

There is only one thing I need at this moment.

"Mummy, are you playing Hide and Seek?"

"Yes, Max. I'm hiding."

That seemed to satisfy him.

I creep into the big pantry, where my stash of chocolate is hidden, curl up with a ridiculously big chunk and cry a bit.

Time rolls on and a whole bar of chocolate seems to disappear, before I hear Jessica's wail.

"I can't find anyone."

"It's, OK, love (the chocolate has made me nicer) I'm here. In the kitchen."

"I can't find Max"

Looking stricken, Finley leaps up and charges up the stairs.

"He's on the roof, Mum… Mum! MUM!"

We're all up there in seconds.

"I must have left my door… I'm so sorry… Max!… Max !"

I can hear a small, wobbly—

"I'm stuck, Mummy. I can't get down"

I can't see him. Finley is out on the flat roof, looking up.

"He's up near the chimney."

Jessica is sobbing. "Max is going to die."

I've called the Fire Brigade. They're only round the corner.

"Hang on very tight, darling. Fireman Sam's coming to rescue you."

Finley looks distraught, as he shouts encouragement, "Hang on, Maxy, you're doing great."

We all hear the fire engine with relief. It does literally come from two minutes away. There are times when I curse the siren's going off in the middle of the night. In this moment, it is the most beautiful sound I've ever heard.

"Hold on really tight. Don't try to move."

"I'm stuck, Mummy."

"Here's Fireman Sam."

Fireman Sam turned out to be Firefighter Samantha and I'm horrified to admit I was worried she might not be as good as a man. This is my son you're rescuing!

The ladder's going up. And she's up the ladder and edging along the ridge toward the chimney.

She's getting nearer…

I'm sure he's losing his grip.

She's talking to Max all the time about how he'll be able to have a look inside the fire engine.

…as soon she gets him down.

And she's holding on to him. She's wonderful.

Another officer goes up.

Between them they're carrying him down.

He's there between them, having the greatest adventure of his entire five years of existence.

They're down.

It's over.

It could only have been minutes. It feels like my whole life.

Max is in my arms and for a couple of seconds there is the most wonderful family hug. Finley and Jessica are both in tears. So am I.

Then, Max is off, tooting his way around the garden.

"Fire! Fire! Nee Naw. Nee Naw."

"Can I have a go in your fire engine now?"

I rush to embrace Firefighter Samantha like she's my favourite Granny reincarnate. Then I remember the two-metre rule and flail my arms randomly in her direction. She smiles and flails back at me.

After Max's new play experience in the fire engine is over, we wave a shaky 'goodbye'.

Our little family is safe.

"Shall we all snuggle down on the sofa and watch TV? I have some chocolate somewhere…"

Turn The Booming Bass Down

Wendy Pike

Relaxing in the garden on a lovely lockdown afternoon.
On the patio, warm and sunny. Birds sing a happy tune.
Boom-Boom. Boom.
Oh no! That irritating loud music's back. Thump-thump, thud, it goes.
Trespassing sound waves. Where they come from? Who only knows?
Boom-Boom. Boom.
Mugging thoughts, sapping energy. And disrupting my good Chi.
Filling, drilling my head. So predictably, repetitive – annoyingly.
Boom-Boom. Boom.
Unwelcome, high-decibel, constant, rhythmic hammering,
Has given my poor ears an undeserved, thorough pummelling.
Boom-Boom. Boom.
Every day, all day. For over a week. Must find a solution.
And quick. What kind of hell is this awful noise pollution?
Boom-Boom. Boom.
I'm no music expert. But is this drum and bass?
Surely the worst sort ever invented. An assault. A disgrace.
Boom-Boom. Boom.
Dear Lord, please make it stop. And make it stop NOW.
No consideration for the neighbours. Such an appalling row.
Boom-Boom. Boom.
Haven't they heard of headphones? They could even borrow mine.
If they'd TURN THE BOOMING BASS DOWN things would be
just fine.
Boom-Boom. Boom.

Can't concentrate on anything much because of the hideous din,
But I am getting some unkind thoughts, occasionally popping in.
Boom-Boom. Boom.
Of how I could make that miserable racket instantly cease,
Stop it stealing my enjoyment. Bring me back some peace.
Boom-Boom. Boom.
I imagine how I could snip the main power lead, maybe?
Or better still, use a sledgehammer to reconfigure their CD.
Boom-Boom. Boom.
But it's only my fanciful ramblings. This truly isn't me.
This uninvited commotion is sending me slightly loopy.
Boom-Boom. Boom.
Considered snitching to noise abatement or possibly the Old Bill.
Having lost the capacity to think straight, not quite sure if I will.
Glorious hum of silence.
Wait. Heaven. It's stopped! Birdsong returns, tranquility restored.
Oh no! Another track. They've just changed the booming record.
Boom… Boom… Boom. Boom-Boom. Boom.

Quarantinis With Bubbles

Yvonne Walus

Lockdown Day -2

Today I felt doubly lucky. Lucky that I was back in New Zealand, and that I had nobody I cared about overseas. Make that: nobody that I cared about, full stop. Except for Ana, my best friend, of course. And Bubbles, my black dachshund. And Josh.

Note to self: don't think about Josh.

Because Covid-19 was the only thing in the news, I anticipated work would be quiet. I was wrong. A queue outside the agency's door, phones already ringing, and I could only imagine my email inbox.

"My mum's in Italy. Can she come home earlier?"

"Should I postpone seeing the grandkids in Scotland?"

"The Silver Muse – both my daughters are on it. How safe…"

My heart broke for these people.

At one-thirty, Jacinda announced Level 4 would commence in just over forty-eight hours. From "stay at home if you're over seventy or have heath issues" to "stay at home" – just like that.

The phones went berserk.

"We don't know what this means for our agency longer term," my manager said as we were closing up. "For now, work remotely. Help our customers."

I didn't have the strength to face the supermarket. Back home, I made myself a drink.

> *Whatever's- in-the-Cupboard Quarantini*
> *1 shot rum*
> *Orange juice*
> *Fresh mint leaves*
> *Verdict: I needed this.*

Lockdown Day -1

Two texts arrived before breakfast. One was from Ana, offering her lounge for the duration of the lockdown. “The twins would love to have you,” she’d said. I adored her kids, but I wasn’t sure four weeks with them was a good idea.

The other text was from Josh. “Spent so much in the liquor store, I got cheered by the crowd. The spare room’s empty and the pantry full. Plus, Bubbles misses you. Quarantine with us?”

Josh and I – it’s complicated. Officially, we were over. He loved bush hiking – bugs creeped me out. I wanted to travel to exotic places – he thought New Zealand was enough. “If I want to see the world, I can just watch *Jamie’s Italy*,” he’d told me. Oh yeah, cooking was another thing we didn’t have in common.

Unofficially, though, I still had feelings. And he still had my dog, because his place – which used to be *our* place for two years – had a garden. So, yeah, complicated. Evening came and I still hadn’t made up my mind.

All-out-of-Booze Quarantini
Cream
Rum
1 teaspoon sugar
Verdict: Meh.

Lockdown Day 0

So, newsflash: I moved in with Josh, just as flatmates. Bubbles went ecstatic and folded himself into pretzels. Josh looked pleased, too.

Felt weird to unpack my rucksack in what used to be our home office. Now it had a narrow bed instead of Josh’s computer, an empty desk for my laptop and a small bowl of flowers from the garden.

Note to self: after a toilet pit stop in the middle of the night, remember not to go back to what used to be our bedroom.

Josh made us drinks in a real shaker, and I felt puzzled by his sudden enthusiasm for mixology. When we were together, he'd have a beer on a hot day, or a glass of wine in a restaurant. We never had a drinks cabinet. Who got him into cocktails?

<u>Chocolate Quarantini</u>
Baileys
Vodka
Chocolate liqueur
Verdict: Not a bad start to a strange time.

Lockdown Day 1

Our travel agency worked around the clock to bring people back home. When I was too exhausted to see straight, I took Bubbles for a long beach walk. We're lucky to live so close to the ocean. I mean, Josh was lucky to live here. I was just lucky to be visiting.

For dinner, Josh made pizza from scratch. Note to self: when choosing a life partner next time, his disinterest in overseas travel should not trump his ability to cook.

We ate in front of the TV, with Bubbles snuggled up between us, like the old times. Luckily, we always agreed on enough Netflix programmes not to fight over the remote.

At one point, our hands met between Bubbles' velvety ears.

"Oh, sorry," we chorused.

Josh got up. "I'll fix us a drink."

<u>Love Potion Quarantini</u>
Peach schnapps
Vodka
Cranberry juice
Verdict: Worthy of its name

Lockdown Day 2 through to 10

Same as the previous day, with a different drink at the end. One cocktail a night during Level 4, that's the deal.

Lockdown Day 11

Ana Facetimed me this morning. I think she wanted to talk about something specific, but she ended up yelling at the kids. So glad I don't have small children. Bubbles totally satisfies my parenting instincts.

Would I want a baby with Josh? If I had to answer truthfully, even if it made me look shallower than a puddle, I'd have to admit that I'd be keen to practise making babies with Josh again. Like, every night. But with a condom.

There.

I'd better have a cocktail to take my mind off Josh.

Chocolate Amnesia Quarantini
Whisky
Chocolate milk, hot
Verdict: Josh who?

Lockdown Day 12

When you reject a diamond ring in favour of visiting Machu Picchu, you don't switch off your feelings when you board the plane. In movies, the heroine is over the guy as soon as she says no to marriage, but reality doesn't work like that. It's not 'we either get married or we break up and instantly stop loving each other' – not when genuine emotions are involved.

I told Ana all this during our Zoom session. Her reply? "So get back together." Like an equation, where X equals Y equals Z. Love is not maths, either.

"Anyway. How are you?" I asked, like I had every day of the lockdown.

"Going crazy."

"The kids?"

"Rocco."

Her husband.

"Can you talk?"

She moved closer to the camera. "He's more irritable than

usual. I know it's one of the symptoms of cabin-fever, but it just feels… I don't know… off."

Everything I'd read about family violence came crashing into my head. "Are you safe?"

She grimaced. "It's not like that. You know Rocco."

Did I know Rocco? He always seemed outgoing, in the loud Mediterranean way that sounded like fighting even when it's just a normal conversation. For my liking, he was perhaps a little bit too jokey with women, but that was a culture thing, right? Josh always managed to be the soul of any social gathering without raising his voice or chumming up the girls.

"So what are you saying?"

"That marriage is a bitch sometimes. Hi Josh!"

I didn't even realise Josh had come home from the supermarket. Just as well we'd finished discussing *my* feelings.

"Hi Ana. Comfy there on our coffee table?"

Meeting friends online meant that 'omfy there on our coffee table' was now the new normal, but that's not what struck me. Josh had said *our* coffee table. Like we were an item.

I liked that way too much.

Later that night, it was Josh's mum on the coffee table. I didn't want her to know we were flatting together, so I hid in the kitchenette, trying to make sense of the dinner ingredients.

"When are you going to bring your new girl around, Joshy?"

My heart stung. New girl? What new girl? The cocktails!

Damn. I never realised it would hurt this much.

"Mum, it's lockdown."

"But you are with someone, right?"

"Yes, Mum."

Regrets? Did I have regrets? If I had my life over again, would I give up South America and marry Josh?

Yes.

No.

Maybe yes?

"Bring her to our family lunch when you visit."

"Mum," Josh said. "Gotta go. Speak later. Love you."

"Bring her home to us."

He disconnected the call. "When I was about fifteen, I promised myself I'd never, ever get married."

"Why's that?"

"My mum's really bossy. I love her to bits, but my whole childhood it's always been *do this* and *don't do that* to my dad. It sucked. I didn't want that life."

"You proposed to me." I honestly didn't mean to remind him. It just slipped out.

"Are you serious right now? You're the least bossy person I know." He walked over and took the knife out of my hand. "Also the least chef-like. Stop murdering the carrots, honey. Sit down and relax. What would you like to drink tonight?"

Honey. He called me *honey*.

Honeysuckle Quarantini
Gin
Honey
Lemon juice
Verdict: I'm pretty sure I'm his 'new girl'

Lockdown Day 19

Another Zoom session with Ana. "He's having an affair," she told me without a preamble.

"Bastard." I didn't ask her how she knew. "What do you need me to do?"

"A big favour?"

"Want me to hill him? Or just cut off his balls?"

"Bigger. Could he quarantine in your flat while you're with Josh?"

While you're with Josh made us sound like a couple. I liked that.

"Absolutely."

She said it was just temporary, how she hadn't made up her mind about leaving him, how children need a father.

I never had a father and I'd grown up just fine. Then again, I rejected a man who would never cheat on me, all because he didn't want to fly over the Nazca Lines, so maybe *fine* was an overstatement.

On my daily walk, I noticed for the first time how eerie the world had become. Sport fields – empty. Beaches – empty. Malls and roads – deserted. Illicit lovers kept apart, ex-lovers shacking up together. Strange times.

Bubbles started sleeping on my bed.

Apocalypse Now Quarantini
Tequila
Vermouth
Baileys
Verdict: I want Josh

Lockdown Day 21

Our travel agency had to close down. During the goodbye bash (online), we played a game. Complete the sentence: 'It only took a global pandemic…' Some were really good, like '… to realise that what I normally buy I don't really need, and what I really need I can't buy anyway', and '… to discover the reason I don't garden is not because I don't have time', and '… to feel grateful for the country we live in'.

My contribution was something vaguely humorous about yoga on Zoom. What I could've written, though, if I were totally honest with myself? That it only took a global pandemic to admit that I was still in love with Josh.

"Are you okay?" he asked when I logged off.

"No."

He sat down on the sofa and held me. "One day, the borders will open and people will travel again. You'll go back to doing what you love."

"I'm already doing what I love," I said. "Don't even care if I ever see Africa." And then I found his lips.

He kissed me back.
Bubbles wagged his tail.

Make-up Sex Quarantini
Shhh…

Apparently My Husband Wears a Dress at Weekends & Other Social Distancing Street Party News

Wendy Pike

(Friday 8th May 2020)

The verbal invitation from number 14 came when Matt, returning from a milk and bread run, bumped into Mike, walking his dog. It was Wednesday afternoon. The call was going out to the whole street: Tea at three in your front garden, Friday, celebrating the VE Day 75th anniversary, if we'd like to join in? Social distancing, of course.

"Shall we go?" asked Matt.

"Well, we've got no excuses. We've got nothing else on have we!" I said, somewhat sarcastically.

So, on Thursday, after we'd enjoyed a fry up breakfast treat (cooked by Matt) our Union Flag was unearthed from the depths of the untidy Tardis that is our shed. Then the hunt was on for the bunting. We knew the red, white and blue was in the loft – somewhere. "I can't be bothered to get the ladder out to find that," Matt got in before I could even suggest it.

There was vague recollection of our daughter's eighteenth birthday party bunting from eight years ago which had been spotted more recently inside the house. And the hunt was on again. Optimistically, smaller, tidier cupboards were searched first and then the realisation hit that the desired decorations were likely to be in the depths of the under-stairs cupboard. Bending low in a yoga-like pose, I dived in over the tinned goods and bottled beer to the far reaches, in the cool box and picnic stuff zone, to have a look. I couldn't find it. Then Matt waded in and not long afterwards, bingo! He came out victorious with his hands clasped around the bag of party decorations, which we both knew had to be in the house – somewhere.

The Hawaiian-style paper lanterns were dismissed as not being in keeping with the theme but the plastic multicoloured bunting, which we had in abundance, was deemed to be perfect, despite it not being the requisite trio of colours. Our daughter Amy decreed it was very fitting indeed as it was rainbow coloured. Unity. Hope. Supporting the NHS etc. Superb.

In preparation, Thursday afternoon I baked Matt's favourite cake. Mrs Pike's famous fruit cake. Famous as the recipe had been sent in to Anglia TV chef Patrick Anthony some three decades ago by my mother-in-law, who also kindly passed it on to me.

A trial run of where and how to hang the flag was left to Matt with help from Amy and Sam, Amy's fiancé.

We ate our dinner later than usual and ashamed as we all are, we forgot it was Thursday and so missed the 8pm doorstep clap for the NHS. I then spent a couple of hours trawling through my vast library of cooking magazines for one of my favourite recipes – custard cupcakes. Persistence pays off. Having searched virtually my entire collection, I did eventually find that recipe – in the third from last magazine in the pile.

We were all set for the street party and in absence of much else going on for so many weeks, also quietly excited for the day ahead, although not openly admitting it to each other.

We awoke with a sense of anticipation and purpose. Something missing from most lockdown days, having had more than a month of Sundays replacing the structure of our usual work routines. And with so much free time on our hands, we were starting to lose track of the days. And weeks.

Very shortly after breakfast, all of us, except Matt, in our PJs, watched as Matt proudly hoisted the Union Flag outside our house, from a long rope tied to the front bedroom window handle and tethered the other end to next door's fence. The weather, already gloriously sunny and warm.

Matt hung up the rainbow bunting around the portico, across the front of the house, over the hanging baskets and along our side of next door's fence, whilst I got busy in the kitchen. On the menu along with the fruit cake: cheese scones, coffee and walnut cupcakes with coffee icing and those longed for custard cupcakes with vanilla butter icing. In readiness I dusted off the two-tiered cake stand, reserved for special occasions only and put the largest mugs I could find on a tray.

We ate our lunch under the shade of the sun umbrella on the patio. Afterwards it was my turn in the shower. Everyone else had got ready whilst I was baking. Over the last several weeks, having mostly been wearing un-ironed jeans and T-shirts, putting on a summer dress added to the sense of occasion. It also reminded me of how much I'd missed getting ready to go out somewhere. And going out to meet people.

At half two, Matt lugged the small garden table, chairs and sun umbrella into position in the front garden. The kettle went on at a quarter to three. At three on the dot, afternoon tea was served on our front lawn. Being generally rather clumsy, I was slightly nervous of tripping over with the cake stand in my hand but thankfully managed to make the short journey from kitchen to garden without incident, everything still intact and edible.

Most of the neighbours were out in their front gardens too. Their homes festooned with flags and bunting along with children's artwork of rainbows for the NHS and the special VE Day anniversary. Yes, it was surreal but a fine display of that typical bulldog-British-spirit in adversity too. And very slightly veering towards verging on mildly bonkers.

Having enjoyed our tea (we soon wolfed it down) I took a walk up and down the middle of the road asking everyone if they'd mind if I took a photo of them outside their home. Neighbours visited each other's tea party, talking to each other from the pavement to adhere to social distancing rules. The police helicopter circled overhead to check we were behaving ourselves. Most of us waved hello before the paraffin parrot lost interest in us and headed off. We weren't doing anything wrong, even if the neighbourhood dogs had no notion of social distancing and the children had dumped any inkling of it, by running around in a pack, shrieking with excitement and enjoying themselves.

Much later in the afternoon, Matt broke out the real ales for him and Sam and a couple of generous double G&Ts for me. Amy stuck with tea. Mindful of the social distancing two-metre rule, we talked to old friends at number 17 that we hadn't seen for quite a while. Them on the pavement. Us in our garden. Vice versa later on.

We met our new neighbours at number one for the first time. I say new. They moved in eighteen months ago. The conversation bounced from holidays and bands to TV and film. On the back of the discussion about Grayson Perry's fabulous lockdown art programme on TV, Matt still hasn't quite forgiven me for telling them he's been known to wear a dress at weekends. I was only joking. Of course, nothing wrong with it if that's what people like to do. Live and let live I say. But our new neighbours were so polite and PC they were happy to believe it was true, their faces surprisingly neutral, not revealing the slightest glimmer of reaction at all.

George next door, in his nineties, showed willing, getting his 70's vibe orange and brown floral deckchair and brown tiled occasional table out in the garden. The oldest resident of the street, George enjoyed a distanced chat with everyone over a mug of tea served from his cosy-covered china teapot. Later, in the warm sunshine and after the first flurry of neighbourly smalltalk, he also managed to squeeze in forty winks, according to Matt.

Mrs-next-door-but-one missed all the social distancing social interaction fun as she had to set off for her shift at Sainsbury's just as the party got going. But Pauline next door had better luck, arriving from her shift at the same supermarket, in time to join in. At dinner time, after persistent clouds of grey smoke, Pauline and family enjoyed a front garden barbecue of burgers and sausages.

As the late afternoon morphed into early evening the temperature dipped. Most people abandoned mugs of tea in favour of a little tipple. But as the alcohol flowed, it became clear that other people's idea of two metres' distance had shrunk considerably and was getting smaller the more they imbibed. We felt it was a good time for us to leave the party.

Once indoors, on went the TV news. The iconic images of a duo of spitfires flying over the white cliffs of Dover and the Red

Arrows flying over empty London streets and landmarks, filling the sky with patriotic-coloured smoke trails, were a massively welcome change from watching the government's gloomy daily press briefings or the day's death toll figures from the dreaded lurgy. Only matched in positivity by Captain, now honorary Colonel and soon to-be-Sir, Tom's inspirational fund-raising efforts in providing much-needed upbeat respite from the usual horrors dominating the news which is itself another victim infected by coronavirus.

We had to watch the Queen's address to the nation on BBC iPlayer. We were outside eating chicken curry in candlelight at the patio table on the front lawn, when HRH was broadcasting her TV message. Her Maj pitched it so well. The speech wasn't overly long nor was it too short. 'Never give up. Never despair,' a sound message for the current COVID-19 situation too, we felt.

We watched an episode of *Have I Got News for You* on catch-up TV over a couple of cups of tea. Afterwards we headed for bed, happily tired, having had a wonderful time. After all, for us it was the most exciting thing to have happened in about two months. The party, having moved venue to number 12's back garden, was still going strong at gone midnight when I switched off the bedside lamp. Apparently it continued into the small hours but after a matter of only minutes I no longer heard the happy sounds of shouting, singing and people enjoying themselves.

All Alone

Gill James

The days of the hacking cough, of the temperature so high that she hallucinated, of not being able to taste or smell, passed at last. They were mitigated by sleep and chicken soup. She was conscious enough to know that they must stay apart, wash their hands, not touch their faces and wipe down everything she touched.

She was almost fully recovered when he started to cough. At least it was safe now. She could care for him. The danger had passed for her. He was still in his separate room and she lavished on him every treatment that she dared. But he couldn't eat the chicken soup, his temperature remained high and the cough didn't stop. He struggled to breathe.

"I'd better call 999," she said.

"No," he said. "I want to stay here."

"Then 111 for advice."

He shook his head. "They'll want to take me in. I prefer to die here."

"You're not going to die."

He turned away from her and fell asleep.

Perhaps sleep was what they both needed. She slept well, in fact, that night, because her disease was gone.

The next morning she found him blue and cold.

The doctor came and then the undertakers, all of them dressed like spacemen. The neighbours stared and then turned away when she looked at them. There couldn't be a funeral but she'd agreed to a cremation. She would grieve later when this was all over. Perhaps invite friends and family to a memorial service.

Now, though, she must concentrate on staying alive. There was plenty to do. All those people to inform, finances to sort out and now she had to do his half of the chores as well. She had her Zoom meetings with her friends and her children. The car had petrol yet for months if all she did was go to the supermarket. Their local store was well organised; it had effective social-distancing measures in place and few shortages.

It would be all right.

Then one day nothing worked. There was no electricity. Her broadband had stopped working. Texts and WhatsApp messages to her grown-up children weren't answered. She ventured out to the supermarket but it was shut and so was the petrol station. Back home she tried phoning her neighbours. They worked for the NHS and had given her their number.

"Just in case we're locked down further and you can't get out," they'd said. "Call us if you need anything."

There was no reply.

She opened the front door and looked out. There were no birds, bees or butterflies around. Even they had abandoned her. No sign of human life either. Was the planet that sick?

She closed the door, took herself to bed and mourned the glorious life she used to enjoy.

A Frivolous Notion

A J Henry

MONDAY

When Cooper left the city, he swore he would not come back. It was his home for fifteen years. On leaving, he declared every bridge burnt. And yet, here he was back again.

Did he hate this place? At one time he did. Now that he was back, the city offered enticements and deception he once adored. Well, perhaps not besotted, but fondness for the gleaming glass facades that concealed an ugly brute beneath. Now, when the virus passed, the city yielded to chaos beneath its hard-shelled surface. The drama of surviving tremors and shocks to the global economy ever present. Concrete pumps throbbed into the night filling cracks between the foundations of office towers. Most nights, he leapt over dirty water in stagnating pools, harbouring dengue mosquitoes. Cooper traversed alleyways to the doorsteps of back street bars to seek solace beneath gasping air-conditioners.

"Share the blessing?" a party of girls in scanty costumes asked. He ordered a drink for a bar girl cradling her face on her hands.

"Does God love this city?" he declared. His shirt clung moist as a face cloth.

"Whaaaaah? For sure she does," the girls chorused.

"Share the blessing?" they sang as he ordered another round of drinks.

TUESDAY

Cooper knew the path. Etched into his memory was a mud map of menace; glassy puddles concealing uncovered manholes; fierce coils of electrical cable dangled from overburdened poles. He leapt to clear green filth seeping from ruptured pipes. He walked to the building site, steadfast in his resolve, wanting no part of the mayhem, the incessant stream of hysterical traffic.

“Is there anything in the city not broken?” he grumbled, his words robbed beneath the cacophony of horns.

A sharp squawk forced him to the edge of the sidewalk. A tricycle driver zoomed along the footpath, teethed bared in a manic grin. His passenger scooped rice from banana leaves as they made their way in the morning commute.

At night, Cooper fortified his apartment with insect spray. Still, they came. He once read American cockroaches were large and black, whereas German cockroaches were smaller and brown. He did not know what these pests were. Cockroaches were a symptom of the city, an adjunct to the warming environment. If they disappeared, would anything change?

Cooper woke in horror. A cockroach nibbled toothpaste from his brush.

On his way to work the next morning, Cooper’s dread resumed. He stamped to scatter a swarm around a grease stain on the pavement. Roaches scuttled between cracks and a pile of rags. He high-stepped a silly jig to avoid the ones coming towards him. Fingers slithered out from under the rags to dip a morsel of food into a puddle. Its skin blackened, fleshed to the bone, limbs shifting under tenuous cartilage.

Cooper guessed it was old, but then, hunger gnaws at human conditions such as dignity. More like a kid, a teenager in a proper life. Its eyes were dead. The thing’s struggle beside a road was of no consequence. Cooper felt a stir of old hatred for this pile before him. Such indifference from gleaming towers, occupants ignoring specs no bigger than fly dirt on the ground below. Knowing such, told him he did not understand this culture, he ignorant of their ways.

It existed (survived seemed too grand) beside the expansive waterway that cleaved the city; a foul river rising in the Monsoon to swoop across levees and drown those living in settlements. Squatters claimed what brief space they could beside the vaulting might of a bridge connecting one side of the city to the next.

Riding in taxis was the worst. It was the colour of Cooper’s skin that attracted them. They came at junctions when the cab stopped at traffic lights. Cooper accepted the urgent beat of tiny palms against the windows. Sometimes he gave them money to which the driver clicked his tongue uttering, *"Sì, tonto de remate!"*

Cooper wasn't discriminating, for God's sake, just asking, that's all, querying why he was the one to notice while the city went about its business. Cooper pulled a bottle of water from his backpack and dropped it beside the wretch's head.

He continued on his way, blocking the encounter from memory.

Cooper was adamant. He was above the herd, not like the teaming thrum of its citizens who clung to this place. He passed a power pole burdened with hand-painted signs advertising 'bed spacers.' Rents in the city were outrageous. Those who could afford a room hired out their bed for those hours they were out.

WEDNESDAY

Cutting across the city were swathes of allotments, illegal settlements that survived through weight of numbers. Rusted iron roofing on make-do shacks scarred the city scape as the ramshackle dwellings snaked between twinkling shopping precincts. Walled compounds shut out the masses. Cooper noted a difference since the last time he lived here. Squatter allotments made way for corridors to build motorways. The residents displaced. City officials believed they would go away.

They did.

Tolls from the disease absent in official records.

"What are you doing?" Cooper asked the bar girls when they stopped dancing. They always quit once the manager went. The manager left to give the *Kapitan* a tribute, protection money to keep the business open. The mama-san should have scolded them, but looked away. The women unhitched their bikini tops and tied them around their heads like lop-sided face masks. They sat along the bar gazing blankly. 'U Can't Touch This', MC Hammer's dance hit, boomed in the background. The mama-san flicked down the volume. The silence was sad, the scene macabre.

"El diablo vive aqui." Cooper said and swigged his beer. Although the virus had passed years before, the women harboured dread, memories taunting them. Other parts of the world called it novel and corona. In this city, the virus translated to 'the devil lives here.'

As Cooper made his way along the path in the morning rush, it occurred to him to cover his face to stifle germs and stench. He pulled his shirt collar over his mouth. As he approached, the kid moved. It touched Cooper (overcome if you must know) in frivolous hope.

He dropped a bag of scraps beside its head along with a bottle of water. Cooper knew better than to expect thanks. The kid wouldn't jump up and pump his hand, saying, "God Bless." That's not how poverty works. He'd seen hunger before. It was wasteful and pointless, and so accepted as part of the human condition of this city.

THURSDAY

Cooper hadn't expected the change. Like so many things in his life, didn't see it coming, didn't think it possible. But what did he know? Cooper believed withered rags lying on the ground to be permanent; a protestation to an unflinching fate that saw the kid there, the cruel repose of hunger. Yet today, the kid sat up, spindly legs collapsed beneath him. The wretch smiled. Cooper tossed him a bag of food, careful not to let its grubby fingers touch his.

Cooper didn't know things medically but this transformation from dull to normal – more normal than before at least – seemed quick.

Frivolous, fleeting hope repeated, "What if he fed this dirt pile? Fed it every day during his stay? Would it unleash the cruel fist of fate that held him? And what if it did? Would it change the pulse of the city and ease the collective conscious? No, it wouldn't. No one in the city would notice, much less give a damn… except for him."

Cooper wondered what his name was? Or even if he had a name, let alone a language. It didn't matter. Cooper decided on a name for him. He will call him Project Boy!

FRIDAY

The Project Boy stood beside a corrugated wall fencing off a construction site. He was waiting for Cooper. Cooper dropped a bag of chicken curry and a bottle of orange juice beside the festering rag pile that had been his home. The kid had a salubriousness about him, a potential to do things. Even though he stood in greasy denim shorts and a slimy shirt, his face held the expectation that hunger would not torment his day, or this day be as shitty as the last.

"Hi," Cooper mumbled. The kid held a grin, as would an assailant hide a flick knife. Cooper knew the kid did not understand English. He felt silly for the greeting. Earlier, when picking up a six-pack of beer from the supermarket, he bought something for the Project Boy in the toy section. A surprise, a plastic tennis racket with a ball attached to a rubber rope. Cooper pulled the packet from his backpack and handed it to him. The kid gazed at the garish coloured trinket. He did not touch it. Cooper could have held a broken lump of concrete, such was the non-response. Cooper was angry at the snub. The audacity of the wretch, turning his nose up at this largesse. A reason for not accepting the toy occurred to Cooper. This kid knew nothing of joy, only hard-won existence and the will to live.

Cooper dropped the tennis racket at the kid's feet, knowing it was, for all the world, a useless thing.

SATURDAY

Cooper peered through the lustrous tint of his apartment window. The sky loomed oppressively. A brooding heaven that sought to redact hopes of a normal day. A sky poised to inflict misery on those below. Wind tore through palm fronds and bent trunks. Billboard hoardings swayed along the highway that ranged over the bridge to other parts.

He watched the weather wash the city of its sins under torrents slithering into every dirty crack and corner. It pleased him. As he listened to burbling window panes before the deluge beating them, Cooper felt snug.

Violent though the gusts were, a tempest toyed within – a gale of playful thoughts. Could he, on this Sabbath, play the hand of God and influence fate? He caught the lift to the lobby.

He pushed a handful of crumpled notes across the counter to buy a three-dollar poly tarp from the 7-Eleven. Grabbing an all-weather jacket, he left amused in knowing the Lord works in mysterious ways.

The avenue was empty. Gone were the rabble and clamour of traffic. Silver droplets collided on asphalt before him as he lurched into buffeting wind. Coconut palms bowed in reverence to the bedlam overpowering them. Cooper pushed on, knowing a poly tarp will offer protection for the kid from the torrent; a make-do shelter for comfort over and above that which the kid had known; provisions of hope for better times.

When Cooper got to the corrugated wall, the kid had gone.

He raced across the lanes, jumping a traffic barrier. He reached a crumbling fence that topped the levee. Islands of weed and lumber swirled in murky currents of the angry river.

Floodwater spilled across the levee and lapped at his feet.

Cooper saw him.

The kid strode across the bridge, dwarfed by the ragging elements around him.

Cooper waved the poly tarp to attract his attention.

It was too far.

He thought he glimpsed a bright thing in the boy's hand.

Cooper waved again.

But it was useless.

The NGO wondered where the kid was going. As rain barrelled into Cooper's skin, a frivolous notion occurred to him, one that was a given in times before.

He laughed.

Could it be this wretch was heading out to find a future?

The Competition

David O'Neill

I swirled the Shiraz around the glass, marvelling at the depth of its redness as it caught the light and letting the rich, berry-like fragrance infuse my nose. It's even possible I smiled as I took a sip, enjoying the plummy flavours and the almost chocolatey after-taste. Pointing the remote control, I trawled the channels on the television, clicking up through them all, one after another, pausing for a few seconds on each to read what it was about, deciding I'd seen it, then flicking up some more. It was just after eight o'clock and I was starting to get annoyed, wondering why I paid so much a month for the service. There were no films I wanted to see that I hadn't already, and many of the programmes were just reruns of old episodes. Nothing new was being made these days due to the pandemic stopping all aspects of normal life, and if I saw another programme where the presenters Skyped in from their bedroom whilst being interrupted by either their partner, children, dog or pet parrot having a loud and squawky wank in the background, I swear I would go postal.

I was about to swear loudly at the television when Jane bounced into the room, her face flushed and her eyes bright with excitement, waving her phone. She had her brown and blond hair up in a can't-be-arsed bun and was wearing some light blue comfortable lounging slacks with that matching top that smothered her ample bosom, which I thought did her no favours at all, but as a man I was biased and I make no apologies.

"You okay, babe? What's up?" I asked.

She took a breath, then a gulp of the wine she had with her and looked at me, blinking.

"You remember that competition I entered, Keith honey? A few weeks ago?"

"You've done hundreds, babe, so no."

"Yes you do, it had that funny cartoon and you had to do a

caption thing. Remember? I wrote," she made a remembering face, "give us a mo'… okay, got it." She held her hands out, index fingers straight and pointing at me as if she was making a really important point, nearly slopping her wine. "Bob promised Joan that next time he would warm the goose fat first." She gave me a set of raised eyebrows, well, if she'd drawn them on she would have, along with a ta-da gesture. I had no idea what she was referring to.

"No, sorry, babe. My bad. But anyway, I'm guessing something's come out of it?" I took another draught of my wine, rolling it around on my tongue and feeling the alcohol warm the back of my throat.

"Something, honey? Something's come out of it? Well, you could say that." She took another deep breath, and another gulp of her wine, composed herself and straightened up into her I-have-something-important-to-say stance. "I've only gone and effing won it." She held her phone out towards me, the screen bright with whatever it was we had won. I couldn't see it from where I was sitting, but she was over the moon, so I was excited for her.

"Wow, babe, that's excellent. We need some good luck at long last. I always knew you had it in you. You're a diamond, babe, a pure diamond. Um, what've we won?"

She put on her smug face, tapped the screen with a couple of fingers to zoom in, moved over to where I was sitting and held it out to me so I could see it. I read what it said and felt my breath catch in my throat, my eyes widening.

She nodded. "Yep, I've won us two tickets, for nine o'clock today."

Panic hit me and I looked at my watch. It was five past eight. "Shit. We haven't got much—"

Jane laughed; a light tinkly sound that stopped me in my tracks. She bent down and gave me a Sancerre-soaked kiss. "Silly. It's for nine o'clock tonight. Finish your breakfast; we've got plenty of time."

My toast was cold by now, so I just drank the wine.

It was nearly seven o'clock and we were both getting ready for our trip out when my phone dinged. I stopped swabbing myself down with the antimicrobial alcohol gel to have a look, seeing a message pop up in the street's WhatsApp group. I would normally ignore most of them as they mainly comprised of bitchy comments about neighbours going out twice in one day, or someone having a BBQ and social distancing wasn't being observed with the obligatory video attached as proof. The fact that they were the same family living in the same house didn't get a mention. And so on. You know how it works.

But this one was from Jane, which was why it caught my eye. I read it with a confused frown.

"Jane," I shouted from the bathroom, "did you post something on the street group, babe?"

Jane was in the bedroom, getting ready since four o'clock. "Yes, honey."

"Was it about how to print out the Non-Exercise Excursion Waiver form, and," I peered at the screen, "how to laminate it?"

"Yes. Why?"

"Well, I did that ages ago, babe. Don't you remember? They should both be on the side by your makeup."

"I know, honey. I can see them."

"Oh, right. Um, okay. No problem, I'll just reply and say I've done them, then."

"Don't you dare," she said, her voice dropping into her deep bite-yer-nuts-off-if-you-mess-with-me tone that made me snatch my hand away from my phone. I'll be honest, my brain went into that confused state that us poor males suffer from on more than one occasion.

"I don't understand, babe?"

"I know, honey. You leave it to me, eh?"

I knew better than to argue, so I shrugged and left it at that and got on with the shave I needed. Looking in the mirror as I scrapped the stubble off, I hoped the tram lines in my hair from the trimmer I'd used earlier wouldn't be too noticeable. I'd used the small mixing bowl to help me get the perfect length all round and then gave myself a number two all over so I thought I looked quite dapper. Better than last time when I'd given myself a number one.

With a mask on I looked like I'd escaped from a cancer ward, so I had to let it grow back a bit.

My phone dinged again, but I ignored it. Then it dinged again, and again, and again, the chimes now coming thick and fast like a pissed-off cyclist. I heard Jane giggle in the bedroom. I'm not sure I got what was happening, but she sounded happy, so I guess I was too.

We did our final checks by the front door. I was up for a taxi if I'm honest, they did special ones for those allowed out, but Jane said we were going to walk.

"Part of our exercise, honey," she explained carefully to me, raising the now painted eyebrows up. Her mask was on, but under her chin ready to be pulled up when we went out. She had dyed her hair full blond again and had used her upside-down drying trick to make it full and bouncy when the right way up. There was a lot of makeup going on around her face to make her looked tanned. It made me feel as if I should have made more of an effort.

"But it'll mean walking the length of our road," I complained. "It's going to take us at least half an hour to get there."

"I know, honey. That's the idea. We should be a little bit early, too, if we leave now."

"Yeah, okay, but that'll mean we have to stand outside as our appointment's not till nine, babe."

"Exactly."

"Well, we might be able to get in a bit early, I suppose."

She gave me her I-love-you-but-you-are-stupid look, reaching up to pull my mask down and giving me a big kiss. "They damn well better not let us in early," she said as she popped my mask back into place, putting her own up too.

I was confused again, which was getting to be the new normal for me. "Okay, let's do the final check, eh? Emergency backup mask?"

"Check." She patted her white leather handbag with the red fluting, colour-matched to her dress, I noticed.

"Latex gloves, and backup pair?" She nodded. "Hand-san?" She tapped her bag again.

"Got yours?" she asked.

I turned so she could see my hip holster. "Locked and loaded, babe. Locked and loaded."

"I like a man who comes prepared," she said, a wicked glint in her eyes, and pulling me close. Her mask was colour-matched to her outfit and I thought she looked beautiful. I won't lie, things stirred. She put her hands up to my shoulders and I felt the lanyard holding the laminated NEEW license drop into place over my head.

I laughed. "You are a tease, babe. But thanks, I'd forgotten about that."

"That's why you need me, honey," she said, patting the licence gently as it rested against my chest. Letting me go she stepped back and gave a little nod towards the front door. I was just reaching out, about to undo the locks when she stopped me.

"Sorry, nearly forgot," she said, pulling her phone out and tapping away at the screen with a flourish.

"Everything alright?"

"Yeah. Just asking the group if the weather's okay."

"Eh? The weather? If I open the door, you'll see what it's like…" But I got the look again so I shut up. I heard my phone ding as it got her message, but I knew what it was so I didn't bother to check it. We stood there for a few seconds by the front door, me still ready to open it but Jane holding a hand out to stop me moving and looking at her phone as if expecting something. Finally, her phone dinged. My phone dinged, too. Hers dinged again, so did mine. Then all hell broke loose as both our phones started dinging solidly for at least thirty seconds. She laughed, putting her phone away.

"Come on, honey, we can go now."

"What just happened, babe?" I asked, opening the front door, the evening sun flooding the hallway with the warm air from outside. Even through the mask I could smell the freshly-cut grass from one of the neighbour's gardens, then I got the rich smoky aroma of a BBQ that someone was having. No doubt there'd be a moan or two on the group about it later. I pulled the door shut and we walked up the garden path, stepping out onto the pavement, the unused cars parked on both sides of the road coated in a thin layer of dust that was starting to shroud their windscreens. The road was quiet and peaceful, no traffic out this evening.

Jane leaned in to me and whispered, "This is what's just happened."

I frowned but then I noticed, following her gaze and looking at the semi-detached houses on both sides of the street, that people were at their doors. I heard clapping and cheering, pots being banged, bells being rung and other noisy things being used. For a second, I thought it was a Thursday, but it wasn't. It took me a moment to work what the day was, and I guessed it was roughly Saturday, maybe even Sunday, give or take. Not that days mattered any more.

Jane waved as we walked along the street, giving me a nudge to do the same, which I did self-consciously. It took me a moment for things to fall into place and when they it did it was a revelation.

"Babe, I get it now," I said, and I'm sure she could hear the admiration in my voice. It all made sense, why she'd sent the messages she had on the WhatsApp group. Damn, but she is clever.

Neighbours were cheering loudly as we walked down the road. I heard my name being called by some of my street-mates who gave me hoots of encouragement, so I gave them a high fist pump and a loud roar back. Jane took it all with a queenly grace, nodding to the women who pretended to clap, their faces sour enough to curdle milk.

We kept to a steady pace, Jane's arm linked in mine as if we were on a royal walkabout. Fewer people were standing outside their houses the further we got from ours, and the noise had quietened this far down the street. Nearing the end of our road, we crossed over to the other side and made for the check-point. Our street's barrier was down this time of night and the community police officers who were stationed there, making sure all journeys were essential, were watching us as we got closer. Jane and I both reached for our passes as we got there, but the officers both smiled under their masks and let us through. News travelled fast, it would seem.

Out the other side of the barrier, there it was, across the road. I felt Jane's hand snake into mine and the pair of us stood where we were, rooted to the spot. Strong emotions were running through me, emotions that I had forgotten about surfacing once again, feelings hitting me that I hadn't experienced in a long, long time.

Jane looked at me. "You okay, honey?"

It took a moment for me to reply. "Yes, babe" was all I could manage, my voice cracking. She squeezed my hand, which helped to ground me. I tore my eyes away from the familiar but also strangely alien building in front of us and looked at Jane, with maybe a tear or two in my eyes. "Best day ever, babe. Best day ever."

"I know, honey. There with you," she said, her voice husky with emotion.

Hand in hand, we walked forward as one. A part of me still couldn't believe it, but it was official, the doors opening as we approached.

We were going to the pub.

The Covid Catastrophe

Katie Ridley

In deepest, darkest outer space, span a peculiar planet, named Corona,
Home to 19 curious creatures, who wobbled, whizzed and whooshed all over.

With their brains full of clever and their bodies bursting with 'pow',
They just could not stand still, not ever, and especially not now.

Dashing left, dashing right, for a game of hide and seek among the stars,
All 19 little covids wandered just a tad too far.

Before they knew it they had completely lost their way,
Tumbling onto Planet Earth on a beautiful, bright spring day.

They wobbled, whizzed and whooshed through every city, beach and wood,
Leaving sticky covid handprints wherever they could.

These handprints were secret, these handprints you could not see,
These handprints were invisible to you and me.

The busy, bustling covids had absolutely no clue,
That the Corona dust on their fingers could make humanlings poorly and blue.

"Look what we've done," gasped covid number 3,
"I can hear lots of humanlings with a cough and a wheeze."

"This will not do," cried covid number 4,
"I can see lots of humanlings hiding indoors."

“We must go home,” demanded covid number 5,
“I can feel lots of humanlings are lonely inside.”

But how would they find their way back to deepest, darkest outer space,
A look of confusion spread across each one’s face.

The humanlings were smart, always one step ahead,
Brilliant bubbles were the answer, or so I have read.

Every child, every adult, in every house and every home,
Blew bubbles from their window, their balcony, their rooftop, their garden or even when out on their daily roam.

There were bubbles that popped, washing every single sticky handprint away,
Then there were bubbles that floated, trapping all 19 little covids and truly saving the day.

Each covid was locked in its very own marvellous, magical and miraculous bubble,
This was the only way to keep them out of trouble.

The sad, sorry covids wobbled, whizzed and whooshed through the sky,
Past the tree tops, birds and clouds way up high.

On and on hurried the bubbles one by one,
Swirling past the shimmering stars, sparkling moon and scorching sun.

Finally, they bumped back onto Planet Corona, with a crash so loud,
The humanlings let out a mighty (?) cheer – they were once again happy, free and proud.

There were giggles, hugs and kisses galore,
The humanlings were kinder, braver and wiser than ever before.

Abi's Birthday Dilemma

Alice Lawes (age 9)

There was a young woman named Abi who had had a child named Kai almost a year ago. It was going to be his first birthday in only a few days and they were in lockdown due to a new virus called Covid-19! I know, a terrible time to have a birthday! Abi, who was a nurse in the NHS, was doing all she could to help people who might have the virus but it was very difficult because she also had young children. She had two wonderful children, one called Mia and the other Kai, who you have already heard about. At first, Mia had the symptoms so they had to be in lockdown. Then, just as Abi had gone back to work, Kai started to have a cough (one of the symptoms) so she was in lockdown again. Abi had been waiting for two weeks now so she could finally go back to work and help out with the virus-infected patients. She's not someone who worked in the hospital but she works in the community (which means she treats people at their own homes).

After her tiring Monday of work, she was putting Kai and Mia to bed when she got a phone call and at first her husband – Dany – picked it up and told her it was the NHS who needed to speak to her immediately. She took the phone and they said that there was a really horribly infected person who was over seventy, she had Covid-19 and was about to die so they needed everyone on the team. Abi told Dany and rushed in the car to the patient and saw that the woman wasn't any ordinary woman, she was the Queen of England. Abi started doing her job, and when she looked up she saw that her teammates weren't doing it properly so she told them to stop and explained how to do it correctly. They got very confused and let her do it instead. Abi got to work while everyone else stared. She was nearly done – the Queen would be healed soon. She worked some more and finally she had finished. They went through a symptoms check and the Queen was now completely cured. They went through another check to see if she was likely to catch it again. According to the results, she was now completely virus free! They all got in the NHS cars and drove off to return the Queen to the Palace. Then they drove to the scientists and explained they had a working method on how to cure people with the virus and which meant they wouldn't catch it again! The scientists were very pleased and told them that they needed Abi to help them figure out the cure. If she could heal patients so they were safe from the virus, she could help make the cure. Abi was very pleased, but just as she was thanking the NHS workers for helping her get to this moment, one of them told her, "I'm feeling very unwell." The others nodded in agreement, then they all fainted.

Abi was alone and was very unsure of what to do so she decided to ring Dany and he came to help her out. They sat Abi's team down in the car and then rang their usual babysitter, who came straight away to look after Mia and Kai. They drove the infected team to the hospital. Abi reckoned they had Covid-19 so she did her thing. Once they were all revived, they started wondering what had happened, and just as Abi was about to explain she heard a huge 'CRASH'. Abi ran to the window (where the crash had come from) and saw a big army of Covid-19 particles! They must have taken over her friends when she was talking to the scientists, and when Esme (the nurse who had felt ill first) had told her she was feeling unwell the particles had then got the scientists! Abi thought the particles were very sneaky and hurried the scientists down to the basement of the hospital to make the cure. Maybe it could stop the particles! They set to work and she told them, "To cure the Queen, I used bacterial wipes, soap and water along with these other things." She indicated to a pile of objects on the table beside her. "I'll show you the rest as we go along." They got on with it and FINALLY the scientists lifted a red bottle. They used a big machine to make a huge amount of the cure. Abi took the job of squirting most of it at the army of particles and they all exploded.

Abi became the greatest hero. She had saved everyone from lockdown and being taken over by particles, and all before her son's birthday too! As a thanks she received a medal from the Queen. It was made out of actual gold! The Queen was especially thankful for Abi's rescue of her and gave her an extra reward, an OBE! It was a win-win for everyone! Abi invited all her family round and they celebrated Kai's birthday, and Kai could say many words now but Abi's top three were "Abi saved us!"

Letter to a Friend

Doug King

My dear friend,

I never thought I would be writing a normal, hand-written letter ever again, having become so familiar with those electronic gadgets that even suggest your vocabulary for you, but here I am putting pen to paper once more. A strangely pleasant experience I had almost forgotten.

I grew up in an era when the Protestant Work Ethic was the national mantra and it was war time anyway. Now, suddenly, the whole nation has been sent home – work from home – don't work – stay at home – don't go out – save our NHS. This is a new refrain that is contrary to all I have ever been taught. So, now I have time: time for anything I please and writing to you pleases me.

For probably the first time since age settled on my bones, I feel sorry for the young (and the not so young). All that energy and nowhere to burn it off. If one has practical skills, one can make things, create items, do those urgent repairs, even re-decorate if the equipment is to hand, even gardening, if that is your bent. But that only fills the first week, what about the other six, seven or eight weeks that follow?

I, on the other hand, I can let tranquillity enter my life. No! I am not going on about esoteric eastern religious practices. That has never been my bag, as you know. Today I can live without imperatives, although I acknowledge I do have responsibilities towards to my loved ones. I will take my adorable dog for a long walk, which we are permitted to do. She will enjoy that, racing across the fields, while in due course, I may regret my kindness when my hips seize up.

Then, I will have my books. As you know, over the years, I have bought many an interesting tome with the promise that they would be read, sometime. There is no doubt that now, at long last, I have the time to read them properly and to absorb as much of the information as I may choose. No one can now lay claim upon my time, because we have been told that we should not leave our homes, so I have no excuse.

Being an advocate of the concept of Life Long Learning, I may choose to make notes of everything that I learn from these books. In recent years, it has often been the young who have taught me new skills and brought new interests to my life. Now I will return to the original skills I picked up at school, taking notes and recording facts to memory, not taking today's short cuts relying on the computer for everything and thereby not understanding the value of anything.

Dare I wish for this situation to continue – no traffic noise, no unexpected callers; however there is still the infernal telephone?

Stay safe, I cherish your friendship.

The Reply

Doug King

How lovely to receive a hand-written letter once again, it takes me back to a calmer and less pressurised time – or was it? Perhaps not, methinks that our memories begin to play strange tricks with us as we age and that creates an idealised remembrance of times passed. If you stop to consider the situation you will realise that while our scientists and others have a better understanding of the causes and effects of the pandemic than we had in the past, they also have far greater hindrances too.

What do I mean by that? I am simply pointing out, in my usual rather obtuse fashion, that for every doctor, nurse or researcher trying heroically to overcome the problems of this virus and striving to nurse the sick, there is at least one non-productive doppelganger employed in the NHS. Those working in administration and finance, where they are busy imposing restrictions, making impractical demands and daily expecting the impossible from their front-line staff. That is apart from them taking out of the NHS roughly half of all the allocated monies from government and interested charities, just to cover their exorbitant salaries. There appears to be Chief Executives in charge of every facet of the medical services many of whom are fundamentally non-productive. One wonders if Watson and Crick would have been so successful in their work, if they had the constraints upon them that modern researchers experience?

But I digress, the thought that prompted this reply to your letter was an increasing awareness that the status quo of our society will be for ever changed by the experiences that we are currently suffering. This virus pandemic and the enforced actions that our society has taken are as much of a shock to our systems of government, as the Second World War was in our childhood. However, for all our recalcitrance and protesting we are still a part of the modern world. Perhaps we should embrace that fact? In many ways it is the people of our generation who were instrumental in putting together the building blocks of modern society. We, that is members of our generation, brought this strange new world into being. I accept that in many ways the recent developments have left us behind, but we still have our humanity to share with others

Perhaps therefore we still have a role. We brought about radical change once, perhaps we may help to do so again. I hesitate on one point – what has been invented cannot be un-invented, so what has become the media society will remain, virtually intact. Perhaps though it may have a more human and caring face than it presents at the moment. The whole experience may help us to regain that which a former Prime Minister dismissed as non-existent – Society.

Please stay safe

They Call this News

Doug King

Over the past decade or so, there has been a subtle but definite change in the formatting and delivery of television news. Not just from the BBC, which is probably the major change agent, but also from Sky News and from ITV as well. Nowadays it is incredibly difficult to decipher what is real news. One has to attempt to decide what is the BBC management's slant on a topic; what is plain exaggeration and sometimes what is, frankly, just lies.

Years ago, maybe through a nascent naivety, the news that was broadcast, especially by the BBC was generally believed. The tenet being that, the BBC, as a self-proclaimed, highly ethical broadcaster, which closely followed the concepts and ideas of its founder, Lord Reith, would not broadcast anything but the truth both in word and deed. How times have changed!

Have you ever played that game, if a game it is, of imagining that you were someone from another planet watching the news channels on television for the first time? It does create a new perspective of the news and its news readers. One can discern an underlying arrogance in the attitude of some of the more experienced news readers and an almost dismissive approach to the reporters sent out from the various studios around the country. It is almost as if they resent the reporter being on screen, taking camera time away from him or her, whoever is reading the news. They are news readers for goodness sake, not prima donnas or great stars in their own right. How the BBC can see fit to pay these people such vast salaries is beyond the comprehension of any right thinking individual.

To continue the theme of the Man from Mars, by watching only the television news channels, but particularly the BBC it could certainly be argued with considerable certainty, that the population of the British Isles is mainly black and/or of Asian extraction. There are very few white persons interviewed and of them significantly few of them are male. Most of the professors at our universities are female and of course we now accept that most medics are female and virtually every consultant is foreign. Well one does if one believes everything that one sees on BBC News. Not that both ITV and Sky are very far behind when it comes to following the BBC lead. The adage being, not white and preferably not male, if it can possibly be avoided.

It must have been a body blow to the powers-that-be at the BBC when ITV News was voted as giving the best coverage of the recent General Election and now with the Corona Pandemic upon us the whole format of news has changed. If one watches just the BBC one would begin to think that the rest of the world has stopped. Apart from regular reports from the USA about the latest silly idea or downright lie from Trump, their esteemed President, the rest of the world has virtually ceased to exist. It has been coronavirus, coronavirus, coronavirus non-stop. It is amazing how they can fill the time with just this one topic. But, fill the time they have, but only at the expense of the last of their integrity. Every newsreel for several weeks seems to have been filled with the weeping faces of people, mainly female, who have lost a loved one through this awful virus infection. The spectacle, every evening, became depressing. But one evening they excelled themselves with their facile banality. They showed an elderly woman lamenting the death of her mother, who was in her late 90s, suffering from dementia and living in a care home. The interviewer asked how the lady felt losing her—

An Overheard Conversation

Doug King

The side effects of social separation and the general lockdown rules during this coronavirus epidemic can be quite strange. A couple of days ago I was in a long queue waiting to be allowed in to a supermarket to do some of my weekly shop. Ahead of me in the queue were two ladies of an indeterminable age, standing the requisite two metres apart but holding an extremely loud and voluble conversation about the television news as presented by the BBC. It was impossible to ignore for two reasons, the first was the volume, which I have already indicated and the other was the topic of their conversation, namely what they perceived as some of the failings of the BBC News Channel, with which, incidentally, I agree.

There was one particular issue that had clearly irritated one of the ladies. Irritated her to such an extent that she had actually switched off the news part way through the programme.

"Did you see that elderly woman on the news last night?"

"Which one was that?"

"The one they did a close up of her crying about her old mother."

"Oh her! Yes I saw her, why do they do that, do you think?"

"Haven't got a clue. I know one thing though, it made me very angry looking at her. So angry I actually switched the TV off much to my hubby's disgust."

"Why was that?"

"She was crying as if she had just lost her child to the virus, but it turns out it was her mother, who had dementia and she'd actually died in a rest home."

"Yes, that's right she had. Her mother must have been over ninety. I wondered why, if she cared that much about her mother, why her mom wasn't at home with her. I looked after my mom at home when she went that way, you know, all that time."

"Yes, you did. I never thought of that. What gets me though is that they keep putting that sort of thing on the news. 'Why' I kept asking myself, you know, like, 'Why her?' 'Why do they think this is news?' and particularly, 'Why did that woman want to show herself up on like that on TV?' "

"I expect she wanted five minutes of fame. Do you think she got paid for it?"

"Don't know, don't care. Have you noticed, every night on the news the BBC have about five minutes, of mostly women, crying about the death of a relative or some such, why? It isn't news is it? I asked my husband about that as well. He said he thought the BBC was doing it for its entertainment value. He said like the Romans at the Coliseum enjoying the spectacle of death. I told him not to be so barmy, but maybe he has a point."

"But what about all those people who have volunteered to help out or come out of retirement to help the NHS."

"Just goes to show how wrong the BBC are on this very point doesn't it? Move up a bit, we are getting near the front of the queue."

"Oh right. Where were we? I know, the thing that worries me is what'll happen to the NHS if all these consultants and nurses that they've interviewed on TV about this virus all go back to their own counties when this lockdown is ended. I haven't hardly seen a white face on the news talking about this virus. Are there any white consultants who know about all this?"

"Don't worry, they won't all go home. Life is too cushy here and the pay is too good. Come on, look, we can go in now to get our shopping."

An Evening at the Masked Ball

Stuart Larner

Getting ready.
Blue satin strapless mermaid dress
shoulder-grazing chandelier earrings
lace-adorned, breathtaking
plunging open back
fitted corset bedecked with
intricate ruffles
flattering my body
silver choker
pedicured toes peeking
tall stilettos
elbow-length velvet gloves
sexy luxury.

My consort
elegant black tuxedo
bowtie
crisp white shirt
formal waistcoat
silver cufflinks with our initials
shoelaced shiny black Oxfords.

To set it all off
this season's must-haves
with unique intelligent style details.
We snap open
the polythene packet
of PPE.
And slip it over the lot.
Covering the neck down to the ankles
these gowns have such a fluid feel.

My mask of fine light blue
covers the nose.
I pull down a face shield secure and clear.
The gown has a generous flow,
a design of meadows and clouds on the front,
semi-transparent so that
my bedazzling evening dress shows through.

My consort has a dragon-style designer mask
and large face shield.
On his gown the Flying Scotsman comes
in full steam towards the observer.

We tie each other's gowns at the back.
Our sleeves have elastic cuffs.
Snapping on nitrile gloves,
we're ready to brave the night.

At the country house
the stewards direct us where to park.
Alternate bays blocked off for distancing.
We enter the ballroom,
plastic-gloved hand in plastic-gloved hand,
swishing and crackling in our gowns.

Beneath the doorman's PPE
I glimpse his major domo uniform
as he scans the tickets on our gowns.
He announces our names
muffled by his respirator mask.
We join two dozen gowns and masks
primped-up plastic flowing
pink heavens and white clouds,
a medley of vibrant colours
art youth culture motifs.

Talk is effortful and garbled.
Once, with no one near, I risked lifting my mask
to consume a canapé
I stabbed with a cocktail stick
issued in a sterile pack.
Our drinks we sip through plastic tubes
from plastic sachets clipped at our sides.

As the band strikes up
only those fully gowned with face shields may dance.
The band's behind a Perspex screen
to protect us from the trumpeter's microspit.
The trombonist slides a blare right out
and thumps the screen.

After we had danced
a gentleman requests the pleasure dressed in full biohazard suit.
Flattered and unable to refuse, I glide
whilst he waddles a waltz Viennese.
Another asks. A forensic
scene-of-crime officer
in white coverall suit.
He has no face shield, so
the doorman moves him on.

In the cloakroom's mirror
a woman gives herself
a throat and nose swab test
to see if she can accept a date.
Another tries on yellow plastic gloves,
posing thoughtful fingers over chin and cheek.
Her friend pulls a face
and offers a pair of pinks instead.

At the end of the evening
the high intensity car park floodlights come on.
We go back to our cars,
rip off our gowns and masks
and put them in the bins provided.
For a brief moment we look at each other
in our dresses and suits.
Slowly the thought occurs
to each of us in turn along the line
that this masking and unmasking
has shown us more about ourselves
than a simple clothing change could do.
That what was underneath it all
is still there,
and beneath the under layers
we are still ourselves.
Then the lights go off
and, as we drive away,
we try to hold onto
what we have learnt today.

What Happened Outdoors

Pam Pottinger

Mum said we couldn't go out to play anymore.
Something bad had happened.
Dad said yes, the blinking animals are going to take over the world.

I looked out of the window
A carpet of cats were already sitting on the shed roof
Purring their song to the sky

I wanted to know when I would see my friends again
If the cats were taking over their gardens too.
Or just ours?

One morning
Mum said, someone had stolen her washing pole.
Dad said yes, my wheelbarrow has gone missing too.

I looked out of the window
It was like a game of I spy
The garden had grown a disguise.

Grass hiding beneath butter cups and daisies.
The path a river of blue stars.
I looked everything up in my flower book

Forget-me-not, foxgloves and floss
Bluebells, harebells and, something else
Big and round and yellowy green growing on top of the compost heap.

Mum said never mind that, come upstairs quick
We all looked out of the window
Dad said blimey, me lawn mower won't like this.

Up every road and every street, over the tops of the buildings
Underneath bridges, twisting up lampposts and telegraph poles
As far as we could see

A jungle of birds and flowers and trees
Mum opened the window
Different noises and smells came in

Bees danced around with a buzz
Hedgehogs snooped and snuffed
Foxes and rabbits and hares were skipping through our town

It was the best thing I'd ever, ever seen.

Until one day it was all over
And Mum said phew, something good has happened
And Dad said, at last, we can go out again. Hooray!

I was glad I could see my friends again

But I was sad too
I wanted to know what will happen
To what's happened
Outdoors
While we've been away?

Isolation

Richard Hough

David (36) a solicitor forced to work from home is using a video link to check up on his slightly rebellious Auntie Mary (72).

David: Hello, Auntie Mary. You've got the camera working then?

Mary: Yes thank you, I wrote it all down when you showed me in February. As you said at the time this might be useful.

David: Well done you. Anyway, I just wanted to make sure you're alright and to see if you needed anything. You're a vulnerable elderly person after all.

Mary: Vulnerable person my foot. I went shopping today. Did you know we had to queue outside the supermarket? The man at the door said we had to keep two metres apart because of "special *{sic}* distancing."

How much is two metres anyway?

David: It's about the height of Uncle Brian lying down.

Mary: Don't talk to me about that drunken, old sod. Anyway I suppose that's about five steps then.

David: You shouldn't speak ill of the dead.

Mary: Weeell, he was a waste of space, always lying drunk on the bedroom floor. He couldn't even find his way into bed half the time and when he did he usually fell out again. Glad he's gone.

Anyway the queue to get into the shop stretched half-way across town. By the time I reached the end, I needed a taxi to get me back to the door. Still, I met a couple of lovely people. We had to shout from a distance just in case we started spitting on each other…

David: Did you get everything you needed?

Mary: What, with all those empty bleeding shelves? I've stopped eating muesli – mainly 'cause I can't find any. I've had to have toast and marmalade since all this started but I don't know how long it's been in the cupboard. I couldn't get any toilet rolls again. It's a good job I'm constipated but God help me when I can finally evacuate my bowels.

David: Too much information, Auntie.

Mary: You'll never guess what, our David!

David: **You've found another man?**

Mary: Don't be bloody daft. I had enough with your Uncle Brian.

David: Alright then, what can't I guess?

Mary: Well, I was squeezing the bananas to make sure they weren't too soft. I happened to look down and there was a fiver on the floor at my feet.

David: I hope you didn't pick it up, you don't know who's been touching it at the moment. You can't spend it anywhere anyway. Please tell me you didn't pick it up!

Mary: Of course I bloody did. I was wearing rubber gloves anyway and I had one of Bertie's poop bags in my pocket.

David: I hope it wasn't a full one.

Mary: I only did that once when I got distracted by that seagull as you well know – AND it was only in my pocket for one night.

David: Yes. Thank goodness I was checking your coat pockets when you lost your glasses otherwise who knows how long it would have been there.

Mary: No, this one was clean. I just picked up the money, popped it into the bag and back in my pocket before anyone blinked. Mind you, no one could see as they were all wearing scarves on their faces. They looked like Jesse James.

David: What have you done with it now?

Mary: When I got home, I gave it a bloody good clean with a wipe and then I put it in the microwave. I nuked the germs, little buggers.

A bloke took the trolley off me when I was leaving the supermarket and do you know what he did? He cleaned the handles with a wipe, right in front of me. I gave him a glare. Cheeky little sod, treating me like I'm dirty.

Here, I saw that old cow Jean in there. She was all smarmy and "How lovely to see you, you're looking well" and smiling; asking how the family were coping. Like she cares. She'd rob the devil if he took his eye off her. I played her at her own game. "I do hope your family is well" and "We must meet up when this is all over." She has more faces than a dice, that one. Mind you she can move for an old girl. You should've seen her scurry off when I coughed accidentally on purpose.

David: You're a wicked old lady, do you know that? Anyway what are you doing for exercise? You know you should only go out once a day?

Mary: I pop up to Margaret's. It's a nice little walk there and back. Lots of lampposts for Bertie to sniff at.

David: You can't do that! You're not supposed to meet up with anyone, let alone visiting your friends!

Mary: Well here's news for you Mr Virus Police. We don't meet up. I take some spray and septic wipes. When I get there, I clean the intercom on the door and we chat using that. Margaret doesn't have a computer and it saves money on phone calls. We've promised to look out for toilet rolls for each other. Anyway, I've rabbited enough about me, how are you coping?

David: I'm trying to work from home but it's not easy with the kids off school. At least they can go and torture each other in the garden.

Thank goodness it hasn't been raining too much this week. It's horrible having access to the coffee jar and biscuit tin all the time.

What with the gym being closed, I'll be like a beach ball by the time summer gets here. Mind you I can't remember the last time I wore a pair of trousers so it's swings and roundabouts I suppose.

[*whispered*] Linda is worrying me too. I think she might be getting broody again. I was only half listening while we were in front of the TV last night but I think she mentioned something about a New Year baby.

Mary: You watch yourself there, young David. You might not have enough money for another mouth to feed. [*chuckles*] I hope you know what causes it!

David: Auntie, I don't need a lesson about the birds and bees thank you; especially from you.

Mary: Well, I'll have to get on. My baked potato is nearly ready. When I've had that with baked beans, I'll need to get out of the house; it can get draughty if you know what I mean. I'll probably take Bertie up to Margaret's. I want to tell her about that cow Joan.

David: [*sigh*] OK, Auntie. Let me know if you need anything. If you feel unwell at all, you tell me straight away. Otherwise I'll speak to you at the same time next week. Look after yourself, bye!

Mary: Bye then, David. Stay out of trouble and mind you don't get anyone else into trouble either. See you next week, love to Linda and the kids.

Closure

Vanessa Horn

Tom forced a smile as he entered the lounge and passed his flatmate a beer. "Anything?"

Luke switched off the TV before taking the can. "Cheers, mate. Nope, no news. Just the usual loop of comedy repeats."

"I wonder…" Tom stopped, not knowing how to finish the sentence.

But Luke seemed to know. "Yeah." Then he lowered his voice. "Have you looked out today?"

Tom shook his head. "Too risky in daylight. I will tonight. But… there's something more important: food stocks are getting low. I reckon we've only got enough for another two weeks, even if we eke them out. And… maybe four weeks of generator fuel."

Luke stared. "Then what?"

Tom sighed. "They'll have to replenish our stocks – they can't expect us to starve to death."

"But no one would be allow…" Luke's voice petered out but then he brightened. "Yeah, they've probably relaxed the rules by now – it's been such a long time. And… maybe the virus has burnt itself out?"

Tom frowned. "Though… wouldn't you think we'd have been told? Or at least heard people outside again?"

Luke shook his head. "God knows. If only the Internet was still up and running." Then he grinned. "But there'll be plenty of people in the same situation as us – everyone had the same rations allotted when lockdown started. So, there'll be something organised. Some sort of plan."

"Yeah." Tom hoped he sounded more convincing than he felt. "Bound to be."

That evening Tom waited until he was sure it would be dark outside and then switched off the living room light. Kneeling by the closed curtains, his hands shaking as was normal when he did this, he peered out of the tiny gap which they'd – illegally – left open. Having that little chink of hope had made the two of them feel less isolated during the past months, knowing that other people were not too far away. It had been a comfort. A support. But now, just as for the last two weeks, when he stared outside there was no sign of life. Just dark houses, unlit streetlamps, empty roads.

Tom sighed. He hadn't realised how much seeing evidence of humanity, albeit just flickers of light and shadows, had comforted him. It, he supposed, just a reminder that people were around, going about their lives, even though only indoors. Luke, too, although he refused to break the rules by looking out himself, relied on Tom to talk to him about the sightings. The reassurances. But now… nothing. What should he say to Luke? Though, was there really anything to say, beyond the fact that he couldn't see anything? Anyone. No signs didn't necessarily mean that people weren't still there. Did it?

He stood up quickly, flicking the light switch back on. No point in worrying unnecessarily. The government wouldn't let them down.

Nearly three weeks later, though, Tom's optimism was waning. There'd still been no sign of food stocks being replenished, or even a message about any procedures which needed to be followed. Now, all that was left in the flat were two vats of water and a few biscuits. He sat in front of the comedy repeats on the TV, formulating – and then discarding – possible explanations and solutions in his mind. Was it time to act?

He looked up as Luke came into the room. His friend had an odd expression on his face. Determination? Belligerence? Tom wasn't sure, but he'd rarely seen Luke look like that before.

Luke's voice was resolute. "I'm going to get us some food."

Tom gaped. "But…" he began, hearing his voice waver, even though Luke's plan was one he'd considered only minutes ago. But it was just a thought. He tried again, assuming an assertiveness he didn't feel. "Is that wise?"

Luke snorted. "What choice is there? It's obvious that no one is coming to help us. This way at least I'll be doing something positive."

"And what if you get caught?" said Tom. "You could be sent to prison… or worse."

Luke shrugged. "At least in prison I'd get fed." Then he laughed. "And have a few more faces to look at than your ugly mug day in day out." He put on his jacket. "I won't be long…"

Tom felt it had been ages since Luke had left the flat, even though he calculated it couldn't have been more than an hour. Immediately after his friend had gone, he wished he'd insisted on accompanying him; even being out and exposed to the virus or the police was surely better than sitting around waiting? But, as Luke had reminded him, there was no point in them both taking the risk. Nevertheless, Tom's thoughts whirled and swirled with worst-case scenarios. Suppose Luke was caught out and taken off to prison? Suppose he became infected with the virus; would he be admitted to hospital or were they still stating that infected people had to stay at home? Suppose… Tom sighed, trying to calm his mind and straining his ears for any sound of his friend returning.

When, finally, Tom heard the key in the lock, he leapt up, running to the front door, his heart pounding erratically.

At first glance, Luke looked much the same as he had when he'd left – just, possibly, a little paler. But – thank God – there were no officials with him, *and* he had a bulging carrier bag slung over his shoulder. Seeing Tom's eyes drawn to this, he nodded. "I managed to break into the supermarket on the main street – got a few cans and things that hadn't gone out of date."

"You broke in?" said Tom, blinking. "But why was it closed?"

Luke placed the bag on the floor. "Everything's closed, mate – it's deserted out there. I walked for miles, trying to find someone – *anyone* – who I could ask what's going on but there was no one a—" he stopped suddenly and looked down, his shoulders hunched. Muttered, "And the smell…"

Tom frowned. What smell? What was his friend not telling him? Then, suddenly, the realisation hit him. He stared at Luke, feeling his heart racing to the point where he felt it would explode. "You don't mean…?" No, it wasn't possible. Couldn't be.

Luke looked up again. "Yes. We're the only ones alive."

Leaving

Vanessa Horn

Amy watched as the sunlight sparkled through the window, highlighting the dancing dust motes. Was today the day? She closed her eyes, feeling the warmth on her face. I could do it today, she thought, surprising herself. If I had to choose a day, it could be today. Then she shivered and opened her eyes, her fleeting courage gone. If only it were that easy. Yet… why not? Why not today?

Now, suddenly emboldened, she rose from the chair and slowly walked the ten steps to the door. She stared down the hallway. If she chose to do it, there were another eleven steps to be walked to the front door. The entrance. The *exit*. Gazing at the shiny handle, she imagined it being pushed down. The door opening. Simple.

Opportunities: they were outside. The things that she used to do… before. Life would get back to, well, some sort of normality, she presumed. Other people had spanned this bridge over the past few weeks – she'd seen them pass by her windows, chatting, smiling – so she knew it could be done. But… had they been too quick in believing the authorities when they said it was safe to go out? *Was* it safe?

Excuses. It was so easy to find them. To be controlled by them. No, she had to do it. Now. Amy took one, then another step towards the door, feeling her heartbeat accelerate with every pace. Okay… focus on the benefits: visiting friends… walking in the sun… Another step… another… a few more…

Trembling, she reached out and touched the door handle. It was cool and solid – something you could rely on. Was she ready? Yes: she *had* to be. Before she could change her mind, she took a deep breath and pushed the handle down…

A Global War

Gerald made his way upstairs, the stair lift was a blessing now. Originally put in for Delia, when her cancer treatment had sucked away all her energy. That was thirteen years ago, it's at times like these he really misses her.

He doesn't mind being alone in the house, isolation was not new to him his nearest neighbour was half a mile away at the end of the track. In truth this is his driveway but the unmanaged hedgerow meant most people drove past without seeing the house sign or his post box.

Being too tired to shower, he cleaned his teeth and went to bed; out like a light.

Woken up by the telephone, grabbing it from its cradle he sat up.

"Yes."

"Hi, Dad, you okay."

"Mathew for God's sake when will you get to grips with the time difference, it's after midnight here."

"Sorry, Dad, I'm sitting in the car, while Lian is shopping, I thought I should check you're alright with virus being global."

"Well you know how isolated I am, anyway I hope Lian is buying plenty of toilet rolls."

"What are you talking about? Toilet rolls?"

"Look it up on the BBC News you'll soon see what I mean, anyway I'm very tired and need to get back to bed, ring again at the weekend at a better time."

"Hang on; I just wanted to say how sorry I am, not getting home for the holidays."

"It's okay; I understand why you couldn't come. Now I'm going."

There is a ringing sound to bring him out of his sleep, taking that minute to realise it's someone at front door. Throwing on a robe, running down to be greeted by Mrs Kramer, the local busybody (councillor) and active member of any organisation you care to name.

"Gerald how lovely to see you, I only said to the ladies of the

W.I. the other day, we'd not seen you in the village lately."

"That's possibly because I'm in isolation."

"Well of course you are! That's why I've brought you a food parcel, and toilet rolls."

He gave a big sigh and muttered what is with people and bloody toilet rolls.

"Thank you but I'm well stocked, I'm sure there's someone in more need then me."

Mrs Kramer had that enquiring look about her, she of all people would want to know how and why anyone would refuse a food parcel. Gerald's quick thinking to avoid telling her of his stock pile of food for the next year in his secret place.

"I received my monthly delivery from the supermarket two days ago so I'm okay for now."

"But you're on my list for a parcel every week, Gerald."

"Mrs Kramer, please! You've got me out of bed and I need a pee, now leave your parcel on the step this time, should I need any help or something, I have the leaflets with all the numbers, I promise to call, now will you go."

The door closed as she lifted the box out of the boot, getting herself as close to the lower glass panel as possible to see inside, only to see the back of Gerald as he hadn't closed the closet door. This was of course on purpose as he had seen her in the village looking into people's windows before knocking on their door. Duly washing his hands, he returned for his box of essentials, there was a moment of delight seeing a bar of chocolate tucked in between the bread and the milk neither of which he needed.

Sat at the table with toast and tea he couldn't help feeling he'd been a bit hard on his son then Mrs Kramer this morning. There wasn't a name for the way he felt, least not in his book. Mathew had a good head on him for all things high-tech. He came home one day saying he was going to Silicon Alley California. After his mother died he didn't come home so often, then he married Lian, he was very much settled in the States. They were due to come over for Christmas, and then Lian's father suffered a stroke so they cancelled at the last minute.

He glared at the list on the fridge, a daily routine of things to do; something to be getting on with at all times to encourage him not to sit around. Otherwise depression will set in, not a good thing when in isolation. It was strange how memories just popped into his head, silly little things triggered the past. How he and Delia had been on holiday here in Devon, when they saw this house for sale. Being exactly what he termed an ideal candidate, she at the time had no know idea why he'd said that.

They went and found the estate agent, made a cash offer and bought the old farm house tucked out of the way on Dartmoor. Delia had so many plans for the interior; Gerald had bigger ideas, an extension on the rear. In the bureau he found all the old paperwork, back at the kitchen table, he spread the contents of the folder out. This brought a smile to his face, as he remembered the man from the planning office saying he could build whatever he liked within reason as the land was still listed as agricultural. With the plans for the extension passed, he set about his masterpiece, Delia was carrying Mathew at the time when Gerald had a very large hole dug about twenty feet deep and the size of a small bungalow.

The nineteen seventies was an unsettling time, as the cold war was coming to a head. Even the government was worried about the nuclear threat from Russia.

He had a fascination for all things made of concrete, ever since he learnt at school the Romans were the first to use it. Of course this had been reason he had to be in isolation; those early years of inhaling cement dust had damaged his lungs.

He made a coffee and crossed over to the pantry door, that's what the enamel sign said but behind was the stairs down to a nuclear bunker, which was under the garden out of sight. After a brief moment looking down the stairs he went back to the table. It seemed odd now that he spent all that money and time planning to protect him and his family and for what? If the war had come about, there would have been nothing left to start a new world. The science said there would have been a nuclear winter and the planet would die anyway. When Mathew was about two years old, they spent ten weeks down there just to see what it was like, as he remembered it was okay but they didn't concede to each other if they could do it for a year. He was still replacing the food down there refreshing it all the time, that's why he didn't need food parcels, he had enough food for a family for a whole year, it had become an obsession to never be without supplies.

He had considered spending the next three months down there. As he had to stay at home anyway! The intention was of updating his information papers for the future generation. Yes a hand-written log of everything, because it seem to be the only thing left you didn't need to replace the machine every other year to do it for you. Of course with Mathew's help all the modern technology had been installed over the years.

Ironically his thinking is different now to how it had been back in the seventies and eighties when he built the bunker, back then all he thought about was saving their lives; he never took in to account what they would do if one of them had toothache or suffered an illness that needed hospital treatment. As he pondered these thoughts one of the many leaflets he'd saved fell to the floor, retrieving it he was compelled to read this information and make the comparisons of what the government had said of what you should do if a nuclear attack was imminent, with what we should do now to avoid catching coronavirus.

NUCLEAR ATTACK. 1 Protect & Survive. 2 You should stay at home. 3 Have a safe room (build a shelter using doors). 4 Have enough food & water for fourteen days plus strong disinfectant & toilet rolls, essential hygiene. If not at home lay in a ditch and cover exposed skin, head & hands. 5 No part of the UK is safe.

CORONAVIRUS COVID19. 1 Stay at Home to Protect the N H S. 2 Wash hands often Essential Hygiene. 3 Stay indoors if you show signs of the Virus. Isolate for up to fourteen days (food needed). 4 Non-essential travel ban, to stop the spread of the Virus. (No part of the UK is safe).

After sorting the papers into some order replacing them back into the folder, he made another coffee and went out to the garden. He indeed felt Delia's presence near the old potting shed, quite often he openly talked to her, taking advice on the plants. The garden had always been her forte; recently he'd been having forty winks on the bench in the warmth of the sunshine, waking up with a start asking Delia if she would like a cup of tea. In some ways he was glad she wasn't here, her body wouldn't have coped with this bloody virus.

He went back inside to look at the list again, reading through the days tasks, deciding that they could wait, feeling an anger that he had to be alone, at a time when he needed to let it out, to put his point of view over and get into a debate how things are all wrong.

Delia had been very good at listening and having a view on all matters; quite often ending with *I'm sure it will sort itself out!* Back in the garden the wood pigeon watched him take the watering can to the tomato plants. The can was thrown to the ground; quick strides brought the bench back into view, like an angry child throwing himself down hard with head in hands.

"Help me! Delia I have to vent my frustration, of all the bloody wars, and the near destruction of the plant, melting the polar ice caps, holes in the ozone layer, oceans filled with plastic, even down to children telling governments how wrong they are is beyond me."

Delia didn't answer; in fact he couldn't feel her presence this time but he carried on.

"The one thing that separates humans from the animals is the ability to talk, communicate in any language and live together, which is what this virus feeds on and could be man's undoing, well I've got that off my chest, now I'm going to lock myself away and do some paperwork."

Mathew spent most of the weekend ringing; the phone was never answered, so he contacted the police in the nearest town telling them of his concerns.

Their return call wasn't encouraging though they gave a contact number of a Mrs Kramer for some reason! It wasn't going to be easy to make arrangements to get home as airports are being lockdown.

June

The Corona Diaries

Boris Glikman

I have never kept a diary before. But unprecedented times call for unprecedented ways of expression. And so, since the start of March, 2020 I have been keeping a diary, noting down my observations of and reactions to the ongoing crisis in the world outside and how it is portrayed via the media, as well as noting down my observations of my inner world and my ruminations on various topical subjects.

Given the dark, gloomy subject matter, I think that the best approach is to utilise black humour, and to portray the events that are taking place in a distorted and satirical manner.

4 March

In Melbourne, Australia and in other major Australian cities, there is massive panic buying, as rumours flood in that everyone is going to be forced to stay home once the epidemic strikes, and that therefore it is imperative to stock up on supplies. Amongst the items that are completely sold out are toilet paper, hand disinfectant, soap and pasta.

5 March

The biggest existential threat facing Australia right now is the absence of toilet paper on the supermarket shelves. And now they are talking about the possibility of an Australian civil war between the haves (those who have toilet paper) and the have-nots (those who don't). I can already foresee that this will go down in history as 'The Great Toilet Paper Conflict of 2020', and that the most important outcome of this war will be an addendum to the Australian Constitution stating that every Australian citizen has the ineradicable right to possess toilet paper, and that no persons and no power shall ever deprive them of that right.

6 March

It has been reported in the news that scientists have just discovered that this virus is unique in that it is self-infecting i.e. it is possible for a person to pass this virus from himself to himself. Therefore, the authorities will now be forced to quarantine and isolate each infected person from himself.

7 March

These are the latest developments in (as I have termed it) The Great Australian Toilet Paper Shortage Crisis of 2020:

To express its gratitude, the Australian government is creating special new medals to honour every worker in the toilet paper manufacturing factories, for they are the true unsung heroes, working tirelessly day and night to save mankind from a fate worse than death.

There will be airdrops to help the worst-affected areas, with specially adapted planes designed to hold up to 1,000,000 toilet paper rolls at one time.

Australian paper money has lost its face value, and has instead acquired, so to speak, 'bottom' value. Its value is now entirely determined by its usefulness as toilet paper. So, for example, a $20 note is now worth $100, while a $100 note is only worth $20, as it is smaller in size and rougher in texture.

Thankfully, there is hope on the horizon, and my faith in the goodness of mankind has been restored, for a benefit concert has just been announced to help all the Australians affected by the toilet paper shortage crisis. Some of the biggest names in rock and roll, such as Queen, Elton John and The Rolling Stones will be playing for free in a one-off concert in Sydney next week. In a gesture of solidarity with Australia, they will perform specially adapted versions of their biggest hits, with lyrics altered to address the crisis. So, Queen's 'We Will Rock You' will be changed to 'We Will Wipe You', Elton John's 'I'm Still Standing' will be changed to 'I'm Still Wiping', and The Rolling Stones will perform 'You Can't Always Get What You Want (But You Should Always be Able to Get Toilet Paper)'. There will also be a special version of that most inspirational hymn of all, 'Imagine', sung in unison by all the performers at the concert's finale, with its lyrics altered to:

Imagine there's no toilet paper
It's easy if you try
No paper towels or tissues
Around us empty aisles

You may say I'm a dreamer
But I'm not the only one
Some day there'll be toilet paper all around us
And the world will wipe as one.

8 March

The Department of Health has just announced that to cope with the ever-growing crisis, the directive of 'Social Distancing' has now been raised to 'Social Panicking'. All Australian citizens are now strongly advised to panic in a calm and orderly manner.

9 March

Holding hands or shaking hands – that once innocuous gesture of friendship or love – has now become a potentially lethal act of aggression and malice.

10 March (afternoon)

During this crisis, whenever I have been going outside into the streets, I have experienced a strange, troubling sensation: a feeling of guilt, uncertainty, insecurity; wondering if I am unwittingly breaking some pandemic-related law or regulation; wondering if the others around me in the street are also breaking the law? It is the first time that I have ever felt the presence of Law hovering over me.

10 March (evening)

The whole world has become a prison. Actually, it is much worse than a prison, because there is no escape. There's no safe haven or freedom anywhere in the world; every inch of the Earth is now a hostile place, containing lethal threats to your life.

11 March (morning)

The Australian government has announced at a press conference that to deal with the toilet paper shortage crisis, all non-essential use of paper pulp will cease indefinitely. This means that there will be no more books, newspapers or magazines printed, as all pulp will go towards the production of toilet paper. Additionally, all libraries, bookshops, schools as well as all private households must hand over every book, newspaper and magazine in their possession, so that they can be re-purposed as toilet paper. According to the government, the usage of paper for books, newspapers and magazines is a wasteful and frivolous utilisation of resources, given that this country is faced with a toilet paper shortage crisis of such life-and-death proportions.

The journalists raised some interesting points with the government spokesperson regarding this new directive. I've noted some of them down:

1) What about Government's own books, such as books which set out all the laws of Australia, and the book which contains the Constitution of Australia? Will the government follow its own directive and hand over those books too? And if so, how will the orderly governing of this country be affected?

2) Will any exceptions be made to books of historical value or to very rare books?

3) Will the government consider extending this directive to other fields of art, such as, for example, paintings and tapestries, which could also provide good wiping material?

4) What about school textbooks – will they also be affected by this directive, and if so, how will the Australian children learn?

5) Can the government advise which books, in particular, make the best, most absorbent and softest toilet paper?

11 March (afternoon)

Following the directive issued earlier today regarding the confiscation of all books, newspapers and magazines, the Department of Science has announced that it is establishing a special laboratory which will test the wiping and absorption capabilities of books, newspapers and magazines, in order to determine which work best as toilet paper, and to rate, according to a strict, scientifically-based scale, the various aspects, advantages and disadvantages of all the books, newspapers and magazines in relation to their usage as toilet paper.

My sole comment regarding this latest development is to note down my realisation of how bizarre and incredible it is that books can satisfy both the highest and lowest needs of mankind.

12 March

Yellow, the colour once associated with cheerfulness, the colour of daisies, daffodils, sunflowers, of Sun itself. Now, its grim historical signification as the colour of disease, of quarantine, of the end of normal life, has returned from the past with a vengeful triumph. Will it ever be able to recover its happier connotations?

13 March

The Department of Communications has just declared that to prevent the spread of the computer equivalent of the coronavirus, all emails and other forms of online interactions must now be conducted at least 1500 kilometres apart.

15 March

I was in the supermarket the other day, and a middle-aged lady in a smart business suit was walking towards me in one of the aisles, pushing her trolley. She gave me a long, odd look and then started screaming at the top of her lungs: "VIRUSES EVERYWHERE! WE ARE ALL DOOMED! THERE'S A VIRUS! AND THERE'S ANOTHER VIRUS! THERE'S NO ESCAPE! WE ALL GONNA DIE!" She then stopped for a moment, gave me another strange look and, pointing in my direction, started screaming again: "HE'S A VIRUS IN HUMAN FORM! I CAN SEE IT! HE IS THE ONE WHO'S CAUSING ALL OF THIS!" People gathered round to look at her but no one did anything.

16 March

The Department of Science has just advised that if you are travelling close to the speed of light, or if you find yourself near very strong gravitational fields like, for example, near a black hole, then space becomes warped and shortened. Therefore, under those circumstances the "1.5 metre social distancing" rule will need to be adjusted accordingly. (It really amazes me how our government has thought of every possible eventuality and has taken into account relativistic situations too.)

17 March

It feels like I am trying to make my way through an endless morass of molasses. There is an invisible yet boundless weight that is weighing me down and impeding my every movement and action, making me feel impotent and powerless against the invisible threat.

18 March

Given that (as I noted down on March 6) this virus is self-infecting, the Department of Health has today announced that to cope with the ever-growing crisis, the directive of "Social Distancing" has now been upgraded to 'Self-Distancing'. To help stop the spread of the infection, all Australian citizens must now stay at least 1.5 metres away from themselves.

19 March

The Department of Health has just issued a new slogan that it hopes will put an end to this pandemic: "Just Say No to the Virus!" What this slogan means is that if you see the virus out in the street, in a shop, on a beach or in a restaurant, just run away. It's as simple as that! Don't let it fool you or tempt you! Don't engage in any kind of conversation or interaction with it! Just run away!

20 March

To help deal with the management of the pandemic, the Australian government has issued strong advice that everyone should at all times carry a measuring tape and a protractor in order to calculate the area of any room that they might find themselves in, and thereby be able to follow the 'One person per two square meters' regulation. This is the formula that is to be used to determine the room's area:

$$\text{Area} = m*n \text{ sine } (a/n-2) \cos (a/n-2)$$

where 'm' is the length of the lowest side of the wall, 'n' is the number of walls that the room possesses, and 'a' is the angle that the adjacent walls make with one another.

The government has also advised that the above formula only applies if the room's shape is a regular polygon. If the room's shape is a non-regular polygon, then its area must be calculated by breaking it up into triangles, via drawing all the diagonals from one of the vertices, and then adding up the areas of the triangles to find the total area of the non-regular polygon.

21 March

There are so many apps for so many different things nowadays: music, games, maps, instant communications… Surely, human ingenuity can also invent an app that functions as toilet paper, or, indeed, an anti-virus app that finds and destroys this virus within the body.

22 March

The Department of Industry has just announced that to save on the vital resources, the manufacturing of 1-ply toilet paper will cease immediately, and all toilet paper from now on will only be zero-ply.

25 March

OK, if no one else will do it, then I will volunteer myself to be miniaturised by a shrinking ray, so that I can go and fight this virus on its own terms.

26 March

The Department of Health has just clarified the confusing and contradictory advice that has been coming from various sources regarding whether or not it is necessary to wear a face mask when you are going outside. The Department of Health advises that it is not necessary to wear a face mask when going outside, except in those cases when it is necessary to wear it. In those necessary cases, you must definitely wear one.

27 March

Paranoiacs around the world must really be rejoicing, as now everyone is in the same boat as they are. Now, everyone is deathly afraid of invisible deadly threats that could be lurking anywhere and everywhere. Now, for everyone, every person in the street is a potential mortal threat to their health, safety and life.

And all those outcasts who have lost their way in life; who have always felt that the world has no time or place for them; who have never been able to make sense of the world; who have been driven crazy by their envy and hatred of the rest of mankind, because all the others had found their place in the world and were happy and content with their lives – well, their day of triumph has arrived because now everyone else is in the same position. Everyone else is now lost and confused; facing an uncertain future; their lives in unremitting flux and turmoil.

28 March

All this panic and hysteria about the toilet paper shortage! Wake up people! The solution is simple and is staring you in the face! Look at nature! No other living creature, be it a butterfly, an elephant, a whale or a dolphin, uses toilet paper. Only human beings (who are supposedly the pinnacle of the evolutionary process) are enslaved by toilet paper.

I propose the following Anti-Wipeism manifesto:

Wipers of the world, unite! You have nothing to lose but your toilet paper chains! Let us wipe out the wiping! Let us be as happy and free as the animals! This is the moment in history when we must revolt against the tyranny of toilet paper, break free from its bondage and stop using it altogether!

29 March

The Australian government has just issued its latest directive on how to cope with the pandemic: Everyone is to lie on their couches all day long and to watch all the news programs, all the special reports, all the updates and all the breaking news about the pandemic, and about all horrible things that are happening to others, somewhere far away in the world. That way everything will be all right and everything will be fixed. The Australian government also recommended covering yourself with a blanket while lying on the couch, as winter is near and cold temperatures are coming.

1 April

One has to admit that this virus does have a morbid sense of irony: Italy and New York, once the quintessential symbols of the joy and boundless vitality of life, of life that never stops, have now become the grim epitome of never-ending death, of death without limits. *La dolce vita* has turned into not so *dolce morte*, and the city that never sleeps has become the city that never wakes.

2 April

If we stop considering this situation from the human angle, just for a moment, and instead look at it from other perspectives, perhaps we might be able to gain some new insights into it.

God: Pandemic? What pandemic? I don't know anything about it and I couldn't care less!

The Past: Ha! Serves you right! You thought you were so superior to us with your cleanliness and your advanced medical knowledge. You thought that pandemics were something that only happened back in the unhygienic, uncivilised past, but now you too are laid low by a microbe!

The Future: So, *that* was the pandemic that got you all scared and shut the whole world down? If you only knew what pandemics were yet to come!

Nature/Wildlife: For countless millennia we have been engaged in a war with a ruthless, relentless foe. This enemy has had countless supplies, countless reinforcements, ever more destructive weapons… For thousands of years, it has been winning every battle against us, massacring our parents, our children, our brothers and sisters, taking over our land and resources. And then one day, as if by magic or miracle, this enemy suddenly retreats on all fronts, if not disappears altogether. We thank Lord God for this deliverance from our mortal, eternal foe.

Coronavirus: I am a superstar, a champion, an absolute legend for the ages in the viral world, for I have taken on an opponent that's ten million times bigger than me, and I'm knocking him down left, right and centre. I have brought all of mankind to its knees!

3 April

In a world that has gone mad, the sane will be persecuted and scorned as if *they* are the insane.

5 April

This crisis is like a myriad swords of Damocles hanging over our heads, always there, threatening to destroy any one of us at any moment, the menacing backdrop against which we must somehow live our lives.

9 April

Those of you who are unhappy about the state of isolation that the pandemic has imposed on you: would you prefer it if the best protection against the virus was to always be in a group of least ten people, at most at an arm's length from one another? So, would you rather be in isolation, or to be always surrounded by at least ten people, wherever you are and wherever you go, at home or out in the streets?

11 April

The experts are predicting that this pandemic will change the world in drastic, far-reaching ways. For example, some of them are saying that once this crisis is over, football matches (in Australia's top football league) will be played on Wednesday nights for the very first time.

13 April

The Department of Education has just announced that it has resolved the endless and inextricable argument regarding whether or not to reopen the schools for term 2, for, by utilising the latest quantum physics technology, it will now be possible to have the schools simultaneously open and closed.

14 April

There are reports that a new range of face masks has just come out to wear during sleep. According to the manufacturers, this mask attaches to your face so strongly that even in your dreams you will be wearing it too, and thus you will also be protected from the virus in the dream world.

I, for one, think this is a great idea, as you cannot be too careful these days, as this virus could be lurking around anywhere.

16 April

If this world is just a simulation that is being run by extremely advanced beings (as some philosophers claim), then in what way could this current pandemic situation be interpreted? Could it be that the advanced beings are getting tired of the simulation in which mankind is the dominant species on Earth? And if so, are they then conducting preliminary tests to observe what the world would be like if mankind is partially removed from it, as in the current situation? Could it be that the next step for them would be to entirely remove, in one way or another, mankind from this world?

17 April

The Department of Science has come up with an ingenious way to solve the toilet paper shortage crisis. After thorough experimentation, it has discovered that if you look at a half-full toilet paper roll through a half-full glass of water, then the toilet paper roll will appear full. Thus, the amount of toilet paper will instantly double! There you go – problem solved by Aussie ingenuity!

20 April

This crisis is making all of our usual, ordinary activities seem frivolous, trivial and gratuitously disrespectful towards the suffering that is going on around the world. So, if our serious activities appear, through the prism of this crisis, to be so petty and discourteous, how would then our activities of leisure, fun and games appear during such a time? Wouldn't any public activity that is inherently non-serious in nature, such as sport, have an inexcusably and irremediably offensive aspect to it? The only thing that seems decent and right to do during a time like this is to stay in a state of mournful stasis and to cease all activities, whether serious or frivolous, until this crisis is gone.

24 April

The Australian government has just announced that the giving of a 100% effort in the fight against this pandemic is no longer enough and that it will, from now on, be giving a 148% effort.

25 April

The Australian government has just updated the announcement that it had made yesterday, stating that the giving of a 148% effort in the fight against this virus is no longer good enough, and that, consequently, it has now increased its effort to 157.548935%.

26 April

All reality is now permeated with a feeling of intangible malice, gloom and danger. Even sunlight, usually a bringer of joy and a lifter of spirits, now has a malevolent aspect to it, for it is bringing illumination to a treacherous, uncertain world.

27 April

2020 – the year that will forever be known as the cancelled year, the year that existence was put on hold, and Earth hung a 'Shut' sign upon itself.

28 April

One unfortunate and unintended consequence of this pandemic has been that people have been spending so much time communicating by Zoom that their heads and shoulders have now become permanently stuck in the little boxes into which they have to insert themselves in order to communicate.

1 May

I've been thinking about how the world will respond once this pandemic comes to an end. Will there be hundreds of thousands of people dancing and celebrating in the streets, à la V-E Day, overcome by joyous relief that it is all over? Or could it be that people will become so used to having a mortal threat looming over them that they will demand of powers-that-be that a new mortal threat be created to hang over them?

Another possibility is that once this pandemic has passed, the next big panic issue to spread around the world will be the recent erratic behaviour of Betelgeuse in the Orion Constellation. Astrophysicists have been saying that there is the chance that it might be turning into a supernova, and the public might demand that the government stops Betelgeuse from exploding and thus endangering all life on Earth with its lethal rays.

2 May

In news it has just been announced that special medals and citations will be awarded to those heroes who have lain on their couches the longest, without setting a foot outside.

Such are the times that we live in now that those who stay on their couches for longest periods of time are considered to be the biggest, bravest, most patriotic, most self-sacrificing and most altruistic heroes of all.

3 May

All happy and positive news is now tainted by the stain of this crisis; no matter how unconnected and far-removed news stories are from the pandemic, they are still contaminated by its presence.

10 May

I think that everyone is likely to be affected by this pandemic, in some way or another. One should try to cope with this crisis as best as one can, with the aim of emerging from it with one's physical and mental health more or less intact. That is the most important thing. All the other disappointments, setbacks and losses will just have to be accepted as a given during this pandemic.

17 May

The upshot of this pandemic will be a fundamental change in our attitudes towards life. As it is quite likely that this virus can never be completely eradicated, we will just to have accept that in life there always are and always will be ineradicable, uncontrollable, unknown and unknowable risks and dangers. We will have to accept that we can't sterilise everything, that we can't disinfect the whole world, that it is a futile task trying to eliminate every possible peril from our lives, and that it is pointless trying to stop the outer world and its dangers from breaching the supposed security of our homes and from affecting our bodies. We will have to accept that anything can happen tomorrow, and that, ultimately, we have no control over life.

20 May

The following commandments were emailed to my tablet from Up Above the other day.

THE FIFTEEN COMMANDMENTS OF THE LOCKDOWN (as the current state of the world is too complicated and too evil for only ten commandments)

Commandment 1: Thou shalt bake sourdough bread, regardless of whether thou hast ever baked before or whether there are plenty of sourdough breads available in the bakeries.

Commandment 2: Thou shalt refer to 'isolation' as 'iso', for life is too short to write it out in full.

Commandment 3: Thou shalt complain bitterly about and ridicule all the lockdown rules and restrictions, while observing them to the letter.

Commandment 4: Thou shalt install Zoom upon thine computer, even if thou hast no one whatsoever to talk to.

Commandment 5: Thou shalt tell everyone how bored thou are.

Commandment 6: Thou shalt catch up on all thy chores and tasks that thou hast been putting off for years, such as cleaning out thy garage, and thou shalt then share with everyone photos of the long-forgotten things that thou hadst found there, such as thy old school uniform that thou no longer fit into, or thy old yearbook, with that geeky photo of thee in it.

Commandment 7: Thou shalt engage the services of a professional photographer to take photos of the sourdough bread that thou hast baked, as per Commandment 1, and which thou shalt then generously share on social media for the whole world to marvel at and enjoy.

Commandment 8: Thou shalt proclaim far and wide how thou hast finally learned the true meaning and value of life, family and happiness, but thou shalt then forget those lessons the minute the lockdown ends.

Commandment 9: Thou shalt tell everyone how much thou are looking forward to going canoeing down the Congo River and climbing up Mount Kilimanjaro, once the lockdown is over, while thou shalt secretly hope that the restrictions are never lifted, as thou just want to lie on thine couch all thine life and watch reality TV.

Commandment 10: Thou shalt go forth and procreate more sourdough bread, for each sourdough loaf baked brings this crisis closer to the end.

Commandment 11: Thou shalt make constant predictions about how the whole world will change irreversibly and will never be the same after this crisis, whist privately, thou shalt plan to not change thy own life one iota.

Commandment 12: Thou shalt tell everyone how thou hast caught up with all thine Netflix backlog, and how thou finally hast had the time to watch all the seasons of that show that was really popular ten years ago.

Commandment 13: Thou shalt pay worship and construct shrines to those sacred objects that are keeping thee sane during this time of crisis: thy couch, thy TV and thy computer.

Commandment 14: Thou shalt create thine own original conspiracy theory to explain how and where this virus really originated, and what the virus' true purpose is, and thou shall spread this conspiracy theory as the only Truth.

Commandment 15: Thou shalt ignore all these commandments and create thine own.

30 May

There is so much fear-mongering going on in the media about the 'second wave' of this virus, that people are now afraid of waving more than once when greeting or saying goodbye to someone. Additionally, the surfers have now become so superstitious that they are surfing only the first, third, fourth etc. waves but never the second wave.

1 June

Maybe only after this pandemic is over will we finally start to appreciate the things that we used to take for granted, for one never really knows the true value of something until it's gone. The value of such things as the sound of laughter in the distance; being free to do whatever we want; looking forward, without fear or uncertainty, towards a bright future; enjoying endless choices in our lives… The pandemic will make us realise what is important in life, what we should cherish, and what are the insignificant things that we can ignore. We will treasure our liberation from the cloud of undefined menace that is hanging over us, and will value being freed from the ambience of amorphous doom that is putting its stamp upon our every thought, feeling and action.

~~~~~~~~
~~~~~~~~

The Authors

A time for clearing out – rooms, thoughts, old ways; deciding what to let go of and what to keep. A pause in a sentence. A rethink.

Sally Angell

Writing enables my thoughts to fly free and allows me to weave them into words.

Angela Elizabeth Armstrong

Educator of students. mindful walker. Inspired by nature

The older generation are as important as the younger generation.

Peter Astle

Writer

I dedicate my stories in this collection to all who have suffered and/or lost loved ones during these challenging times. Please be safe.

Jim Bates

Now that I'm home, I feel fortunate that I'm not living permanently alone during this pandemic.

Phyllis Burton

Life is never going to be the same…

A.S. Charly

Forging friendships and community spirit.

Jo Dearden

Fiction writer

Lockdown? A time to catch up with yourself and reassess priorities.

Greg Duncan

Living in a pandemic has brought new meaning to the word: discipline.

Susan A Eames

Travel and fiction writer

Writing gives me the conduit to a world that is unreachable by any other means – a world that is populated by Eternal Truths, Ineffable Questions and Infinite Beauty.

Boris Glikman

Writer, poet and philosopher from Melbourne, Australia

Either keep on rocking in the free world or roll with it. Thanks.

Doug Hawley

Reaching out to others in unexpected ways. We can't touch but we can stay close.

Misha Herwin

Writer

I've met my neighbours for the first time and learnt their names as we all look out for each other.

Richard Hough

A perpetual dreamer and optimist

Humour can alleviate the harmful aspects of Covid, be it an amusing character mask, a cartoon in the paper or a comedy sketch. It is good to see people trying.

Janet Howson

Writer.

A time for reflection and learning to enjoy my own company.

Gill James

Shielding, fiction-writer, editor, publisher

Never before have I thought so deeply about what it means to be human, nor about the importance of cooperation, consideration and care.

Dawn Knox

Writer, fortunate to be shielding with her family

To find the positive in the negative.

Stuart Larner

Reclusive writer

Learning to take one day at a time and accepting that what will be, will be.

Linda Lewis

After a dark time, in lockdown, I rediscovered the wonders of nature and came out into the light.

Joy Mawby

The First lock down was a time of fear and a time of calm for me, a time to be still and to dig deep and to revitalise by keeping my spirit moving.

Maeve Murphy

Wife, film maker, short story writer, novella creator

It's amazing how social distancing has brought us all together.

David O'Neill

Novelist, short-fiction writer, ICT and Clinical Systems Consultant for the NHS, but mainly a proud Dad and Granddad

A change in the world but will this change the world?

Val Owen

Elderly scientist who watches the tide ebb and flow while writing

I miss most a hug from loved ones

Colin Payn

Better times are ahead.

Michal Reiben

When we all learnt the importance of…toilet paper.

Hannah Retallick

Writer, editor

Finder of knowledge forgotten, passion and patience revived – for homeschooling purposes.

Neta Shlain

Parent, screenwriter, poet

The world of tomorrow is made by the effort of today.

Ray Suchow
Educator, writer, author

2020. When we realised what really matters.

P. A. Westgate
Indulging in an eclectic mix of activities

I miss the sound of laughter. I'm grateful that I can write.

S. Nadja Zajdman
An author who lives alone

www.ingramcontent.com/pod-product-compliance
Lightning Source LLC
Chambersburg PA
CBHW060625310726
48982CB00003B/678
* 9 7 8 1 9 1 0 5 4 2 7 2 9 *